UNSTABLE

QUERENCIA PRESS
MMXXII

Querencia Press – Chicago, IL

QUERENCIA PRESS
© Copyright 2024

ISBN 978 1 963943 33 7

.

www.querenciapress.com

First Published in 2024

Querencia Press, LLC
Chicago IL

Printed & Bound in the United States of America

contents

Never Ending and Sudden – Alex Carrigan (he/him)

—After Millicent Borges Accardi's "Let's Very Often Say"

It is never ending and sudden, but lasts for years.
Trauma clings to you like moss on a stump, overtaking the injury.

    The injury may have stopped bleeding, but the
    scar threatens to open if you trace along it.

You trace along it with a cotton bud, hoping it's
gentle enough to not bring back the intensity from that day.

    That day was the last time you remember feeling healthy,
    the last time you remember your mind was free of static.

Static threatens to pour out of your ears if you tilt your head to the
side, so you cover them in hopes you have built a strong enough dam.

    A strong enough dam may be enough to contain the
    ricochet inside your gut, but only if you remember to plaster.

You remember to plaster the cracks, having long since accepted the task.
It is never ending and sudden, but lasts for years.

Alienation & Hue – Gwendolyn Harper (she/they)

Baby look into the camera
no it'll be fine, it'll keep you safe. In
my hands the camera is safe, a safe place
creating safety, building strength, strong backs,
we are making a most resilient nation
we are making
we are making ourselves

...
we are making ourselves
fat, thin, old, experienced, very brave for one
so often so completely chickenshit.
Did you even wince that last time he hit you?
NO, we took it on the cheek, we didn't even feel or react
save inside—but there was no longer care, or concern, you hit me
hooray, now what? Who cares.
You're the dumbass obviously for hitting a fencepost, a tree, the side of a building
some aluminum siding. IN inanimate and quiet object that is sometimes used by others for hitting

Now girl, that's a trip, not what we came to rip a tide, dial nine for what was

my actual point then? We aren't here to talk about the past though of course, we are all always free to do so especially when it helps, for we must still sometimes bleed, apply a leech, maybe three, get it out, drain this psychic pus, use those thorns, thorns and wasps and bees, use them all to wick away, to clean it off of me.

We are making ourselves

less of a pack of victims. More than just survivors. We, we crowded hollow children are safe in our dying husk, we are the only strange things here crawling around inside, and we shall keep it that way. We are our own corruption and rot so that no others can get in, no toxicity, no sin. Goddess and cum will sluice that all away, through you, a vessel, a channel, a canal not a well.

Stagnant waters, be so mean, strangling you with killing, uncurrent, holding still, stasis.

We did not come here to discuss dying, deathly, swimming with vines burrowing their seeds up inside of me, it makes me happy you see, when we depart there will be flowers here, growing from death seed

We did not come here to talk of drowning in this life, surrounded by toxicity and all inhaling its fumes WE are trapped but we stand triumphant, triumphant but in our own shit, no chase Manhattan no cash money to get out of this pit. The walls change but the depth of your burial is always the same

We must liberate what is left inside and let it out to see before the world kills itself and takes all options but death and survival away from you, me, and we are making a death-bow, taking our final performance. In twenty years this will be extinction, so who cares, let us out, let us taste of sweet freedom, let us play, let us have the god damn signal we want to hold the power before stupid men kill us all with their unimaginaity

the r1b haplogroup is the most mostest rapey

pie speaking rapey mother fuckers, a tac nuke and a time machine, fix the world, eat berries, not death-panic at the high voltage gay barbarian

we are
We Are <Making
We are making ourselves
WE are making ourselves over while the room is burning, the house is falling apart, and the city is flooding.
We have no other options. Open the phone, no one admits the water is in their own home.
The water is underneath everything. And the crickets shall follow.
We are making our way out of here. We are making ourselves a door in the air to a land of no leaf blowers,
sound pollution, rules and regulations, beauty standards, mediocrity. Freedom from all that we see.
We did not come here to speak of all these dying things but we needed to be honest, it doesn't really matter
No one is listening, no one reading, no one considering
beautiful twentysomethings covered in tattoos and everything
having that you will never achieve
do not care about such things.
WE WANT TO BELIEVE
But mostly
We just want to leave.

Most sincerely

some of the most VERY angry children you have never seen

Who's Afraid of Pronouns? - A Theoretical Cento
– Audrey T. Carroll (she/they)

ideology:

Borrowed from French idéologie, from idéo- + -logie (equivalent to English ideo- + -logy). Cognate with, but not derived from, idea. Coined 1796 by Antoine Destutt de Tracy.[1][2] Modern sense of "doctrine" attributed to use of related idéologue ("ideologue") by Napoleon Bonaparte as a term of abuse towards political opponents in early 1800s.[1]

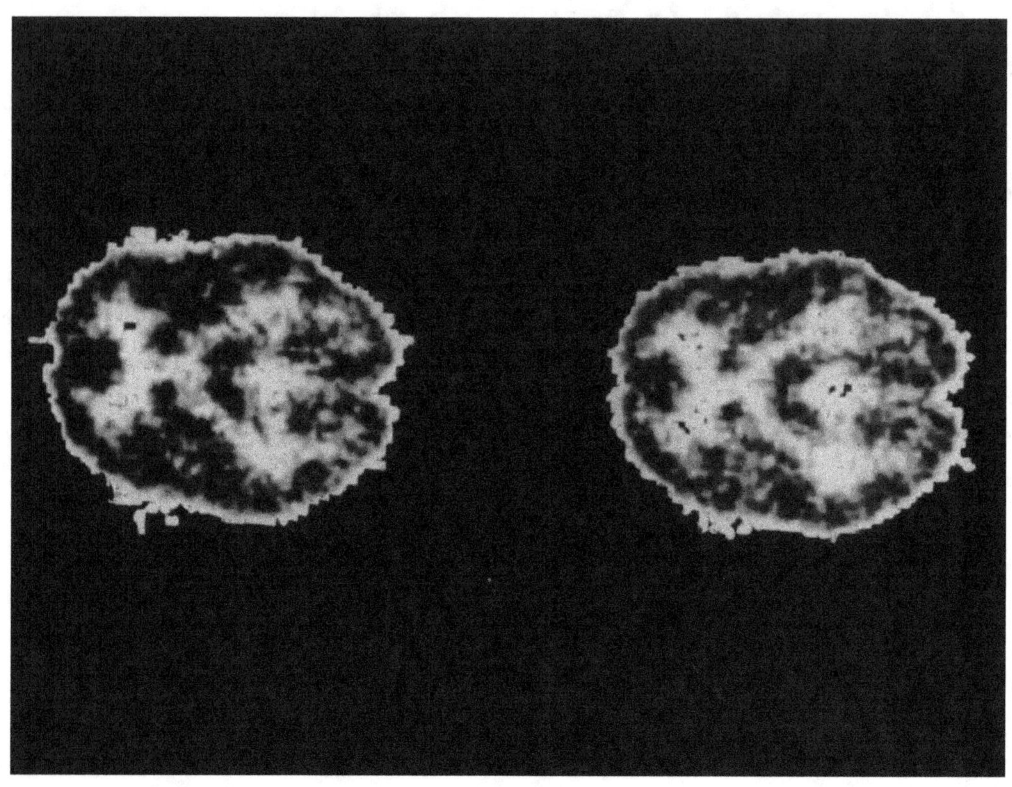

In the 90s we got commercials about your brain on drugs. We need new commercials about your brain on woke gender theory. Cuz uh I'd prefer someone who's brain was on drugs to whatever this is

---

[1] https://en.wiktionary.org/wiki/ideology

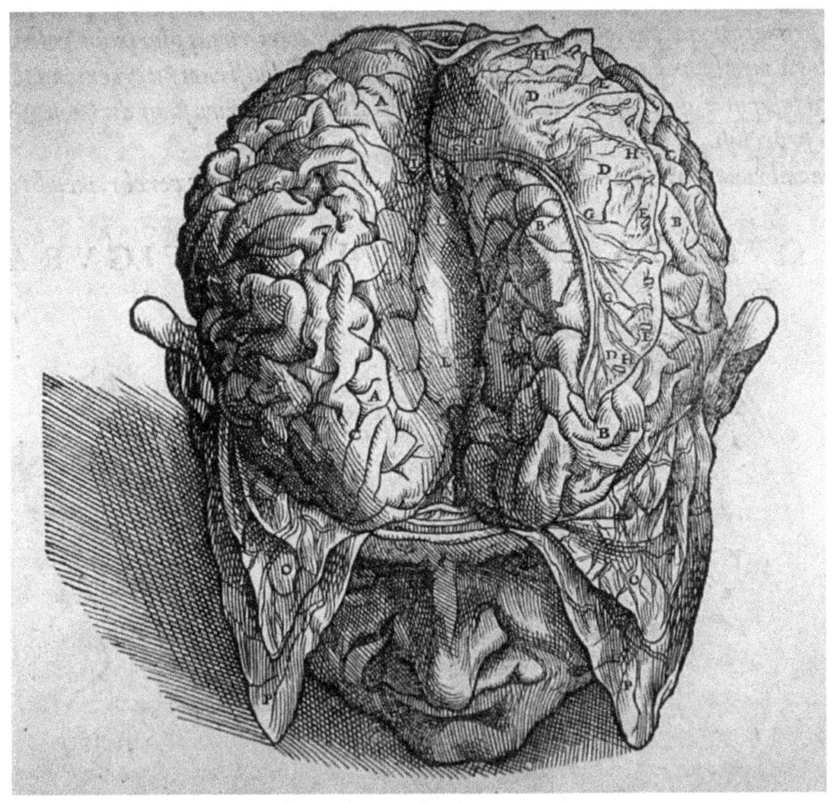

There have... been legislative and policy rescindments, restrictions and punitive approaches leading to criminalisation of certain corporeal and speech acts for LGBTIQ+ people depending on jurisdiction and institutional setting; as politicians perceive the value of 'political homophobia' and 'gender ideology' (anti-transgender and anti-woman sentiments) and anti-intersex sentiment for authoritarian and populist state building [30, 31]. These may be harmful influences weighing LGBTIQ+ bodies down with negative sentiments and potentially influencing or restricting potentials for euphorias.[2]

Social movements such as feminism can provide the ideology and impetus to question existing arrangements, and the social support for individuals to explore alternatives to them.[3]

---

[2] Jones, Tiffany. *Euphorias in Gender, Sex and Sexuality Variations Positive Experiences*. Palgrave Macmillan, 2023.
[3] West, Candace and Don H. Zimmerma. "Doing Gender." *Gender and Society*, vol 1, no. 2, 1987, pp. 125-151.

████████my son like dolls
and pink.... He is still a boy. My
daughter liked blue and truck.
Eventually they outgrew those
things and have changed what
they like a 1000000 times kids
are meant to develop and grow
and learn but it is more so
shown as like he wore a dress
once his name is now lily and
now on hormone blockers. Fix
the media. Fix the propaganda
and the child abuse. But it's
ok because the population is
going to dwindle over the next 3
years dramatically because of
everything we have let happen
because we are a Nation
Divided because everyone is
out for themselves. I miss the
90s

Fredd's case made for a riveting documentary, and although the BBC interviewers did not push in these directions, questions about childhood cross-identification, about the effects of visible transsexualities, and about early childhood gender selection all crowded in on the body of this young person. What gender is Fredd as he waits for his medical authorization to begin hormones? What kind of refusal of gender and what kind of confirmation of conventional gender does Fredd's battle with the medical authorities represent? Finally, what do articulations of the notion of a wrong body and the persistent belief in the possibility of a "right" body register in relation to the emergence of other genders, transgenders?[4]

---

[4] Halberstam, Jack. *Female Masculinity.* Duke University Press, 1998.

emotional manipulation and lies don't work with me. 👍 That's the job of the parent, and it's creepy .pdf file gr00m3r apologist language to say you need to talk to children and confuse them by introducing concepts beyond their comprehension. But I understand your side thinks #loveislove - because all roads of "queer theory" end in calling children responsible, able to consent little adults. #genderideologyisharmful

The #metoo movement—begun in 2006 by the antiviolence activist Tarana Burke—has also helped reveal the ubiquity of straight men's sexual violations of women. Numerous high-profile and well-loved men have raped women, drugged women, exposed their naked bodies to women, and masturbated in front of women without women's consent and with impunity. By 2017, the tidal wave of these stories was enough to make even the most jaded lesbian feminist ask herself again, *What the fuck is wrong with men?* and *How and why are straight women surviving heterosexuality?* You deserve better, girl.[5]

---

[5] Ward, Jane. *The Tragedy of Heterosexuality.* New York University Press, 2020.

no doubt in my mind but I will
not cater to people who take it
beyond the trans and turn it and
twist it influencing children who
don't know anything but what
we teach them. My problem is
the future generation of kids
is doomed for those raised
improperly. It to each his own. I
did my job.

Combined, when looking to discourses of age and future, one's value and one's purpose is continually driven and framed through the young, the next generation. For many, this likely feels like an inherent good, after all—yes, Whitney—"the children are our future" ("Greatest Love" 1985). And queer kids face obstacles that are real and important. But as an underlying narrative logic, this commitment is inescapably tethered to the systems of straight time and temporality in ways that devalue age and aging queers. Baked into this cake are governing systems of procreation, generativity, inheritance, and "proper" maturation.[6]

Stop the abuse of children who
cannot consent to life long changes,
even if they are asking for it.
#genderideologyisharmful

Online encounters might be more likely these days, but science fiction's texts and fandoms still offer lifelines to weird kids and adults who need more narratives of sexual and gender identity than their immediate worlds can offer.[7]

---

[6] Goltz, Dustin Bradley. "Rhetorics of Gay Future and Queer Futurity: Strategies of Disruption." *The Routledge Handbook of Queer Rhetoric*, edited by Jacqueline Rhodes and Jonathan Alexander, Routledge, 2022, pp. 413-420.
[7] Lothian, Alexis. *Old Futures: Speculative Fiction and Queer Possibility.* NYU Press, 2018.

blockers and synthetic cross
sex hormones are not reversible,
they have devastating long term
effects and make a patient
out of these people for life.
It's abusive to not tell them
"my love, my child, no." THAT'S
parenting. The hard part - telling
them that self harm and the
lies of #genderfeelings are
true. Gender Ideology preys on
them when they are emotionally
and mentally distressed, uses
cult tactics and language -
then harms them in irreparable
ways. If I can cause one person
to question it even a little, It's
worth it.

Compulsory schooling has been prolonged further since Firestone's era and current economic conditions make it more difficult for even more privileged young people to live without parental support (Jackson 2010, 120), and anxiety about children's safety and development seems to be at an all-time high.[8]

I believe no one is listening to you
because you are only speaking
nonsense. Your empty and lost,find
GOD!

---

[8] Robinou. *Queer Communal Kinship Now!* Punctum Books, 2023.

My family, despite its cisheteronormative exoskeleton, grew fleshy interiors that kept the queer daughter, the genderqueer cousin, the gay uncle, and the polyamorous folks close to the heart. This was the family that taught me to forge kinship outside our caste, class, and religion, to make others part of our family; to perform the caring labor of kinship for anyone who sought it.[9]

> I really don't get or care to understand all the gender
> ideology stuff. I usually just ignore whiny people/
> trans like that, but most of my hobbies are better
> done alone. Btw Does anyone know the episode
> where they compare a trans woman to a therapist
> finger banging a woman in the 20s?

---

[9] Prasad, Pavithra. "In a Minor Key: Queer Kinship in Times of Grief." *QED: A Journal in GLBTQ Worldmaking*, vol. 7, no. 1, 2020, pp. 113-119.

People who make these social transitions-often termed "transgender" people-disrupt cultural expectations that gender identity is an immutable derivation of biology (Garfinkel 1967; Kessler and McKenna 1978). In social situations, transgender people-as all people-have "cultural genitalia" that derive from their gender presentation (Kessler and McKenna 1978).[10]

Using a pronoun made from English
language is like using a broke condom

A cognitive factor that is correlated with ambiguity intolerance is essentialism (Lee et al., 2020). Defined as the belief that social categories have stable and fundamental characteristics, essentialist beliefs about sexuality and gender influence both bisexual (Hubbard & de Visser, 2015) and transgender (Ching & Xu, 2018) prejudice. This may be due in part to the stereotypes pertaining to bisexuality and transgender identities playing on the perceived ambiguity of both (e.g., assumed instability and gender nonconforming behavior).[11]

---

[10] Schilt, Kirsten and Laurel Westbrook. "Doing Gender, Doing Heteronormativity: 'Gender Normals,' Transgender People, and the Social Maintenance of Heterosexuality." *Gender and Society*, 2009, vol. 23, no. 4, pp. 440-464.

[11] Arcieri, Amanda A. and Lacey Rose DeLucia. "Development of a Scale of Prejudice toward Bisexual and Transgender Individuals on the Basis of Ambiguity Intolerance." *Journal of Bisexuality*, vol. 22, no. 1, 2022, pp. 1-29.

FUCK YOUR PRONOUNS.... THERE ARE
MEN AND WOMEN THAT IS IT ACCEPT
IT IT'S BEEN THAT WAY A OVER
BILLIONS OF YEARS..... YALL JUST
GOT BORED AN ENTITLED

Think about how gender norms, or ideas about what men and women should be like, might be being enforced in your classroom or in other parts of your life. What does it mean to stand up against the rules of gender, both at work and in other areas of our lives? How might we be enforcing gender norms on ourselves or our loved ones with well-meaning advice or guidance? Exploring these questions can deepen our commitment to gender self-determination for all people and to eliminating coercive systems that punish gender variance.[12]

---

[12] Spade, Dean. "Some Very Basic Tips for Making Higher Education More Accessible to Trans Students and Rethinking How We Talk about Gendered Bodies." *Radical Teacher,* no. 92, 2011.

Caught in Weeds – Kim Malinowski (she/they)

Anxiety chokes out flowers
                clenching melancholy in weeds

Hanging onto self
                dandelions gasping scent of mowed grass
                                anxiety in the weeds

gripping hands around neck
                even while dancing...the weeds prune.

Whispering violently
                trembling—soul shattering sobbing
                                kneeling in weeds

Fevered thoughts
                agitated, clutching, trapped in weeds.

Tide Chart – Lawrence Miles (he/him)

High Tide
1AM

The heart tightens
The stomach punches from within
The beads of sweat on the brow
The dull light of clouds dollop the stars
I am afraid if I slumber
I will wake to an abandoned world
Of mass rejection
The spill of the toxic indifference
Authority touching the ceiling and proclaiming
"Who let you into the room
And when will you show yourself the door"

Low Tide
7 AM

The sun has arrived
The heart has finally loosened
The light slowly burns the shadows away
The body needs to sleep due to overnight acidosis
But the day needs to start
I do not check for any communiques
For I do not trust myself
Nor what my reactions would be
Sweat covered shirt comes off
Ritual shower is fulfilled
Try to keep it steady as the day begins

High Tide
1 PM

Hearing it loud and clear now
Nobody else around
I look out a nearby window just to make sure
There is not a mob outside
But the choir picks up the tune
"We want you to go away now, please
We do not care how you do it

We were just too lazy to notice before
But you cannot hide in the shadows forever
Now choose any one of a thousand doors
And get scarce"
Low Tide
7 PM

The sun is ready to say goodbye
But the fog is not ready to lift
I should check the memorandum now
But I would rather give the heart its rest
I make sure the bedsheets do not need changing
Then I start charting the tides for tomorrow
Noting time to breathe and time to sweat
Time to walk away from windows and to drink fluids
Time to know when to enter slumberland
Time to know that the world is not always against you
But only if properly charted...

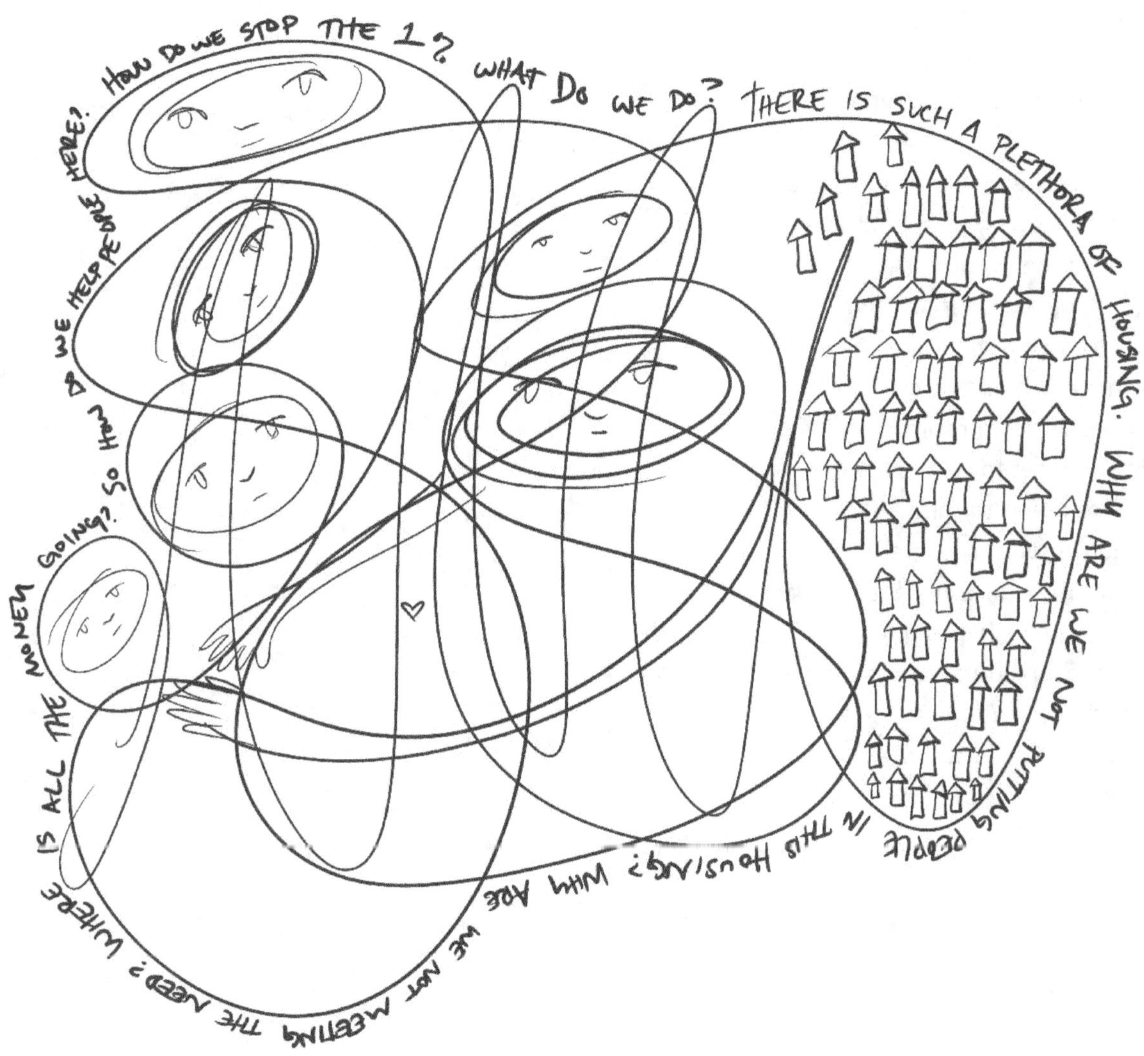

HOW DO WE STOP THE 1?
WHAT DO WE DO?
THERE IS SUCH A PLETHORA OF HOUSING. WHY ARE WE NOT PUTTING PEOPLE IN THIS HOUSING? WHY ARE WE NOT MEETING THE NEED? WHERE IS ALL THE MONEY GOING? SO HOW DO WE HELP PEOPLE HERE?

Hang Up – Angel Rosen (she/her)

"If wellness is this, what in hell's name is sickness?"
— Amanda Palmer

Thorned lip sat on a questionable jaw chasing
empty certainties, opening the
ground with my nails, pulling away
the posies at possibility's casket.
I spear any cardinal out of the tree
so this scene can't be mistaken
for something beautiful, everything
is too connected for me to escape,
this/that netted beneath me. I still hear
Lily's voice alive in my phone telling me
that she loved me on purpose.
I still feel her hands offering me disgust,
hating me for loving her
in the criminal way she devised.
Her act set with my improvisions.
I became sharp set for a sorry horror.
A simple face aging to thirty—
takeout menus for pillowcases,
she plans to drink for three straight days,
whisky chasing my shapes down.
In our last conversation I said *call your doctor*
and she said *I have but what's the point*,
there is no way I can get better
and not hang up this phone.

Bug Brain – Emily Rose Miller (she/they)
     —golden shovel after "Bug Like an Angel" by Mitski

I'm always moving forward until I'm not. There's
no way to predict the halting, trudging like a
gnat I found in the butter dish the other day. I'm bug-
ging now more than ever before—I thought I could work at something I like
but my brain's ant-trails figured otherwise. I'm an
expert at worming my way out of labor, pleading angel
baby, busy bee. Next time would always be different. But I'm still stuck
in my hypothalamus right as it's time to buzz, to

fly. When I was a child I was taught not to be like my aunt; the
threat of not acting a carpenter ant, of unpalatable mental illness—that bottom-
shelf disorder that keeps a body from work—had a chokehold on my family. Of
course, I struggled with something acceptable—medication can fix *my*
sticky web-brain. Depression can't mean dysfunctional, here, but my glass-
cracking hive-mind didn't get the memo. I don't know how to live with
whatever this sting really is even though I've been doing it my whole life. Then, there was a
reasonable deniability—*I'm normal, I can be a good worker bee, just give me a little*
time. But that was the whole illusion, my moth eyespots gone in an inevitably ending bit.
Here, at the end of my web with no more illusions, I don't know what I have left.

Clinomania – Jessica Swanson (she/her)

and true, it's an innocuous first step—
neither gun nor pill, but a small thing,
like a pen knife to a chrysalis
just a small slit to free a reluctant butterfly
all it takes is a few hours of extra sunlight
and a smiling face, asking:
you like the sun, don't you?
don't you?
aren't you grateful for what i did?
you like it—warmth? the warmth?
never mind the crumpled wings
ill-formed, even
i helped you, baby
it's time to fly now
you know you didn't even need to ask
because i've got your best interests at heart
you, weeping scales across an underdeveloped social scene

and i admit i kin as the bear wedged in the back of the den
six months out of the year, warm and safe and unbothered
who doesn't have to shower or get up for work the next day
and smile or chat at whomever graces her existence,
lest she forget social cues to mama bear's chagrin—
a tired millennial of a kodiak

and it's not really so bad, is it—
it's not the big, gaping maw of a d-word with that big capital d
it's not, really
it's not
if i'm able to do other d words, like dress and daydream
even if i'm partial to other words, like disassociate
or damn—even if i don't really have one to give
because this last one, it might be mine

i'm free to devour—to dream away—my own free time

and rawr, babe, i kin as dragon too
my bed, a hoard of pillows
with a wealth of blankets for my little dragon claws
who even sent you on this quest

when there's actually no princess to be had?
and what do i get out of it
aside from some kinda cool scar?

draw your weapons and leave them
at the bedroom door

memento mori on the dance floor – jp thorn (he/they/any)
—with a line for jane from charles

here's a fun date idea:
let's play bingo
with the periodic table,
'lots left on my bucket list plus
have you tried mercury mixed
with a bit of scotch?

you'll be pulsating plutonium,
ringer silent, lips on vibrate
tiny fisheye cameras
in our technologies
watch bodies twine
into square knots,

breath circulating in tandem
hexed by musical drone, its bass
thrums my chest & i just
wanna didgeridoo you all night,
weather permitting, see

       if you can flood the floor
       the way i make it rain
       we'll lull the storm inside
       my apartment,
       gnash & grind & dance against
       probable of electrocution,
       inside this penthouse on stilts
         it's grease lightning,
         hydroponic
         automatic
       spit & sweat, too.

dog tongued, jaw agape with agápē
       i'm a lovestruck loon;
anyone who moves like that
could never die. insomnia
resents routine, so as you sleep
i scrub floors, walls, windows, ceilings
reset the viscosity back

sacrosanct, well-practiced
belief through monologue,
especially the idioms i've
muttered over, now time worn

      don't put it down put it back

things i'm actively using
end up lost in between
unfinished thoughts.

i check on you once an hour,
confirmation bias
that tonight ends with
some form of company,
in this room the hours of love
still make shadows
until every black & blue
shoved from the sky
morning elbows through
to cast a spotlight
on the fantasia,

          cheap memory
          foam mattress
          pressed with your shape
          sleeping curled, fetal
          fossilized memento mori

it is often thought
that depression equates to sadness
but i have found
that depression depletes all feeling
leaving emptiness in its place
painfully craving any emotion at all
but finding nothing
and you feel it coming on,
that void
trying to reverse what you know
is quickly approaching
desperately grasping for happiness,
for anything,
with numb fingers
not even feeling the moment
it slips away

@mysoullaidbare

Lesson for the Teacher – Melina Cohen-Bramwell (he/him)

This story could end with me
soaking my feet in undiluted bleach
till the skin welts and
boils like pasta water
Popping bubbles of amber flesh
Clean to the bone

In Emergency wishing I could go home
they'd say *I'll send an email to your psychiatrist*
and I *could you try not to if that's allowed*
As if the crowd hearing it absolves me of
meaning the opposite

My mom gave me a rubber-band
and I've been snapping it so hard
every time I think to slit my wrists
that it's left bruises
I want you to see

what you did to me
You left me hanging for a week
and now I'll from the curtain rod
the shower leaking behind me
drip drip dripping the time wasted
putting words in your face you'd never say

Do you **see**
what you did
being nice
then stopping
when I told you what nice meant to me

How can I show you so you understand
that it was you who ran the potato peeler
over my wrist
to make fragile crisps of me
That it was you not me
How do I show you
so they all can see
People are such visual learners

Crowned in Cold Iron – Jordan Seireil NicShuibhne (she/her)

*"Thig an smeòrach, thig an druid
thig gach eun a dh'ionnsaigh nid;
thig am bradan thar a' chuain
gu Là Luain cha ghluaisear mis'."
—The Seal's Song*

I

Her legs are spread astride the fjord,
feet firmly rooted in the frozen ground;
the trees arise between her toes, their leaves
tickle the soft skin between them as they grow.

Ghaoil a phiuthar, I'm sorry.
Growing up is a cruel joke, told by God,
who waits in the breathless space between
the darkness of the set up
and the lightning of the punch line, staring
at you, self satisfied, smirking.
Blue light bathes the black forest
for only an instant, only long enough
for you to make out the shadows
of the iron bars over your window.
"Where am I?" You whisper.
Cackles crackle like thunder
across coal black storm clouds,
a churning burning avalanche cascade
of pyroclastic sorrow.

Where you are is an empty room,
the walls are gray flat stone.
The mortar between them is rough enough
to wear your finger's flesh away if you scrape it
or scratch it. You do, anyway, because in a prison
mortar is like a wound. It itches.
You leave your blood behind, wet like paint between the stones.
You look up. There is a window
you could fit through,
if you were tall enough to reach it.
But when you are tall enough to grasp

its ledge with calloused fingers
you will be too big to fit through anymore.

II

    She is the Goddess of Youth, Persephone.
    Her chest is as flat as the eastern steppes.
    Her navel is filled with deep blue rainwater
    and her skin is slippery with morning dew.

Phiuthrag sa phiuthar, I'm sorry.
The storm began long before you were born,
but he sheltered in your dry harbor.
Is this what it means to be a God?
God hands misery to God,
until pain is branded
indelible in the darkness
between stars struggling to flicker, to be seen
through wisps of clouds that, like smoke,
float away on whispered lies.
Zeus passes on misery to you, he whispers
"if only I could tell someone, then I could stop,"
he whispers, "I could stop, if I tell anyone."
As your father leaks out of you
like oil from a wounded earth
you stare, seeing nothing and everything.
He tells no one.

III

    Upon her brow she is crowned in black rings
    of cold iron, heavy as Hades kingdom.[13]
    Its coarseness presses into her scalp's skin
    as her growing skull strains link against link.

Olympus rain comes flooding into your gray room.
It comes up to your ankles when thunder claps the ground.
Earth Quaker, Light Maker.
He stands outside your fairy mound,[14]

---

[13] In folklore, cold iron can be used to contain or ward away supernatural creatures.

clutching his belt as if he were dangling
over a great fire. Maybe it is the last
thing holding him up. And are those tears?
He gets out of his car, his shoulders are heavy
with grief, with pain. His face twisted
by needles of desire. They wrack his body
like a seizure.
You are old enough now to see Kronos
in those tears. To see that as he walks
up the driveway, he steps in Ouranos' shadow
leather shoes crunching
gravel into smaller gravel, mixing
tears with the driveway dirt, thinking
of whatever it is you did that justifies what's coming.
Love slams you in the chest with five open fingers, a palm
that rattles your ribcage, singing
a low and smooth tone. A moan.

You love him. You may not mean to but you do.
It was simple, when you were younger. Now
you are just tall enough to touch your fingertips
on the windowsill when you jump, to get
a look at frostbitten treetops against a winter sky,
and that love feels like a disease. A wretched fever.
Starved to anemia.

The door opens.

IV

    Grown too big for her crown, her skull fractures
    like shattered tectonic plates. It splits open.
    Her blood splatters across the sodden hillsides,
    a mudslide of gray matter lost to rivers.

Ghaoil a phiuthar,
I should have hidden you between the earth and sky,
where he could not see you.
Nach truagh leat fhèin nochd mo chumha?

---

[14] A fairy mound, or fairy fort is a circular stone structure in folklore, said to be the dwelling place of a supernatural
creature, or a portal to another world.

Now there is no world left for you. Should you become
a frigid old woman, sitting in a dim lit kitchen, clutching
a single cigarette between two shaking fingers
as you ask your son, why do you do this to me?
As you ask him if he hates his mother,
if he stays out all the time and drinks and parties
to hurt you. "Am I a bad mom? Did I do something wrong?"
He'd say, "no mom, it isn't that at all,
no, that's not what it is at all."

Your memories are like a needle
pointed at the corner of your left eye.
You cannot look at them, or they will
perforate your eyeball, open
the skin like a white grape with red veins
and you will stand there clutching the edges of your kitchen sink
while the bounteous spring you made taunts you from outside
your window, and instead of playing like a child in the blooming fields
you will scream into a drain. And scream again.
"Where am I? Where am I?"

And when you wake up, you'll feel steel
  picking your rib cage, opening your crucible
    and you'll look down and you'll see little people
      walking in and out of you. Their arms are full of fuel.
        You are paralyzed. It's happening again, it's happening
all over again. Your shriek shakes the firmament,
"They're eating me! Oh god, oh father, please help me,
I'm sorry, I'll be good this time. I promise."

And sometimes you'll find your own gray room,
just to sit in it for a while, just to feel
not safe. Never that, again. But safer.
You want to go back,
that's the cruelest joke. You miss him.
But you are a goddess of the earth now
and when you stand on the highest peaks
of frigid mountains, where winter never ends,
and reach for Olympus, you can only just manage
to situate its distant image between two outstretched fingers.
It looks so safe up there. It looks so peaceful. Why
did you have to grow up?

V

    Mortal men, who seem like ants on her vast mountains
    saw through her blood drained femur with machines
    and drill into her breasts for blackened milk
    that burns upon her skin as bright as sunlight.

And now I am a banshee,
wailing at the forest edge near your fairy mound
Hù rù. Hù rù.
You placed one bare foot outside of it, testing toe first,
and then walked with swaying purpose out into
the moonlit forest, shrouded by shadows
of branches and tree trunks, your red hair
like curling licks of fire around your head.
The roots gnarled, foot catching in their sweetness,
but you knew them. They knew you. You were springtime,
the cruelest season, bringer of life and death,
and you had come to the forest crucible.
The waiting buds all stood at attention
for their Queen, whose head was crowned in cold iron,
to give the command. Birds looked up from southern
lands, listening. Dens, in anticipation,
waked their sleepers, opened, and let them forth.
Branches reached to trembling lengths for their own stars.
And through the forest came whispers waiting for
the season to strike all life like a clap of green thunder.

Instead, you have a blade
that gleams with obsidian moonlight.
You lift it, and the earth is breathless.
You point it at your needle-eye. You cry, "die, God."
And, edge in hand in hand, you push
that black knife's tip into your open pupil. Your mouth
is pried wide in silent screaming as it pops
and the sound of blade scraping bone rends the air.
as the knife goes past your socket,
and when you fall to your knees,
the world is arrested by a never ending winter.

    And then, they are all gone. The carved up landscape

barren of humanity's last whispers.
But the lake is a diamond in her navel,
and her legs are covered with deep green moss,

and birds light on trees that grow from the empty
sockets in her skull, singing a song older than
language. They sing, *all who die are martyrs
on life's cradle. Gone but never truly lost.*

The body not as a checklist of abstract concepts,

Ariele Costantino (he/they)

The body as a fleshy thing that
exists right here, right now.

This body of mine is a specific body.
If i lived fully and happily inside of it, i dont know what that would
say about me.

The body as the location where personal triumph occurs. The body
as a nexus of opportunities for pride.

The body, empty shell of layers

I should learn to locate my body in space before i start demanding
things of it.

Living is not the same as writing poetry about it

Me in the same room as baby me singing to it boy youre gonna
carry that weight

I did not sprout wings

yes i will live i will live i will live yes i can breathe i can breathe i can
breathe
a girl whos all thumbprint into a boy with no name and in between
a wingless creature, living in secret, gasping for air

13 years old kissing my iphone thru an app

I said "nothing is happening over here, put me on another
channel"

To You, Mariposa Minority – Brendon Blair (any pronouns)

tell me the high-strung songs you keep
locked tightly in glittery boxes
on walls and mind-palace centerpieces:
desperate, dauntless, diverse, dizzying in flight

some were like butterflies, their gazes flitting
their needs and yet still trapped between bars.
the world is struck by what they wished for.
what do we wish for?

those deep-seated stories always
keeping you on high winds and yet
grounded in our shared sensibilities:
weaknesses, emotions, desires, needs and not wants

that someone would plant flowers, not pins on a wall,
that somehow we'd find a place to rest.
i wished for what we all did, of course.
another way to ease my torn wings.

some complexities obviously scar
we forget somewhere down the line
if the road puffs up, becomes fire-red,
the forest is not destroyed, it begins anew

FOR LUCY
FOR LUCY
FOR LUCY

can   you   love

                  anything

   without   loving   the / the / the

ONTO GOD

         almost   everything

can   you   learn   possibility / possibility / possibility   NO / NO

      always   there   ENDS / ENDS

                  LOVE / LOVE / LOVE

without   unlearning   HATE / HATE / HATE   AND

                  HASS / HASS / HASS

      arriving   NEFRET / NEFRET / NEFRET   NO

why   do   most   powerful   words

uproot   from   fear   ?   BEGINNINGS / BEGINNINGS

can   you   love   anything

without   loving   THE SERPENT / THE SERPENT / THE SERPENT

can you love anything at all ? darkness the loving without

can you love anything for the tides to shift waiting untied not tied loose forever knots

The Shitpost Poem – Eileen E. (he/she/they)

I can feel the word
Cringe hinged to your tongue waiting to leap out anyway
But I'll hit you with this truth
Love Breeds Innovation.
I know. I know.
And I know it.
I have many cynical bones in my body.
I too have had many hopes and dreams degraded by the machinations of society
Hierarchy before people
Tradition before people
Profit before people
In societies that have been so warped,
As to become cancerous, growth for the sake of growth
Who cares what happens to everyone else?
So long as I get to be one at the top?
I know and the world will not let me forget it.
Even in the cold realities made manifest in my day to day,
I still laugh when some person has the gall to believe:
CApitAliziM brEEdS InNOvAtIOn!!!11!

reclaiming the title 'the alchemist' – jp thorn (he/they/any)

i've been studying lessons in chemistry,
how to dilute a belief system or synthesize an orchestra;

lesson four:

set timers and dinner tables to calculate wholeness;
watch bread form in the oven, the way a family gathers
to gossip over a meal. prerequisite, the control & variables;
mix temperature with pressure & maybe some chemical x,
missing blossom, bubbles, & buttercup. cut the stem cells,
arrange a bouquet in a test tube that resembles a vase,
results seemingly a happy accident though i manipulated
the outcome in sake of nostalgia.

*note: do i seek an outlier only to find myself staring back,
a ripple in a petri dish?*

lesson three:

seedlings pressed wet against paper towel basking on
trite window sills, a simple example on creation of life but for
some, this is all that comes next. trial & error, tweaked out set
periodic table of elements, results published post mortem titled
'final will & testament,' left behind for kindred mongrels to sort
out your original sin. i don't agree with that scientific method;
here my laboratory is replete with self gathered samples: use
them to generate house beats & luxurious garments, little hugs
for one to get lost in the complexities of sound waves & silky
threads, those nights you go out glossed up, wildly perennial.

lesson two:

precious gemstones are now manufactured in my laboratory
so i may never want again. self-appointed experts argue replicants
will never merit authentic stones, i say *who cares enough to note
the difference?* in an age of information turn away from sponsored
conclusion to favor of organic truth, novel archaicism
crafted from method meeting vulnerability, where one is
naked but not afraid, fertilized eggs frozen by the thousand
await a real estate market crash to chance that hole-in-one,

the womb ironically our first address.

note: some never recall it as home.

<u>lesson one:</u>

my first little ramshackle had holes in the ceiling where fluid
would leak, i rotated tiny orifices as buckets so that it could
never overflow & wash me out. nine months. a body's ability
to protect itself—uncanny. the reptilian desire to live is almost
shameless, what thing just regenerates a limb or survives 27 stab
wounds. we're struck with persistence of vision, chiseled into an
unrecognizable marble thumb with no fingerprint, relief shapes
greco-roman figures; dying gaul, winged victory,
a broken hymen rekindling the torch of calliope.

<u>conclusion:</u>

our universe might have been the first lesson in chemistry
& who's to say it didn't explode. there's beauty in the breakdown,
lesson in trial & scripture written erroneous
no need to jot it down & preach when teaching is within,
intrinsic then internalized, soundwaves of screams
embryos overhear as drumlines—they imprint,
another uncontrolled variable from that original lesson on life,
how to manifest two distinct human halves whole,
not a new life
for your old burdens but
how to create a person layered
yet unheavy, balanced featherweight
able to navigate brutalism
effortless, umbrella in the rain.

Leftovers from My Death – Devon Neal (he/him)
—After "Warriors of Love" by Iris DeMent

Even now, in the stillness of my inaction,
a mirror of the sky unheard in some trees,
I wish I could put myself under that bulldozer
in her place, listening to the sounds
of my sockets separating, ribs snapping,
the machinery of my life ground to dust.
I'd want to watch every second of myself
cracking and spilling into dirt, all for the sake
of standing against hate. And after,
I wouldn't stand and walk as a gentle spirit.
I want to see love bloom along every shore,
no matter where, to see families walk
together with roots joining further roots
in the deep belly of the hot earth
that sees no difference in our walk.
No, let me be the angry spirit
that acts as a cancer to those possessed by hate,
let me burn away the racism red in the immune system,
squeeze the organs dry, twist the bowels,
let me poison the ideas, drain the cash
that feeds the systems and their hunt
for the families, trembling in their homes,
their only sin the sin of ancestry. I want to sing
with a burning candle at the night sky,
to hold a posterboard sign with black letters
on the skittering stream of the local news,
but more than that, I want my leftover spirit
to move like a black wind against shuddering trees,
tearing out the white-hot roots of intolerance.

The Starling – Marie Elizabeth Thomas (she/her)

Psych ward phone cords are shorter
Than the ones in this movie
And the chairs are heavier
So no one can throw them

They don't let you have shoes with laces like that, either
And the nurse makes you raise your tongue

So you can't hoard pills and OD like he did

Why don't moviemakers ask those of us who've been in psych wards
Before they write movies about us
And produce them with so many falsehoods?

Is it because these movies aren't made for us
the movies about madmen and madwomen

They're made for the others, who've
Never resided in psych wards
Never sat through eight hours of group every day
In rehab

I'm not sure whom these movies are made for
But it certainly isn't us

Couldn't Make It To The Hyperfixation Meet. – Brendon Blair (any pronouns)

so here's a (mildly) short list of what i know and believe to be true:

i do not need to be captured to
be understood. the idea of me
muzzling myself for modern
society is utterly disingenuous.
i belong to the two-headed cows
in the endless fields out there, not
made of reeds or wanting, anymore,
but taking. i can't keep making
masks every day to stay afloat.
'progress is some island i swim
to at low tide.' yeah, RIGHT. now
i know the strength of the waves.
i missed the meet but i hope
you guys were there. & i
hope we decided to be animals.
biting, feasting, howling,
like the sweet creatures you are.
panting heavy, devouring every
last bone of information,
wet strings of change,
sinews of evolution.
each thing that we can fucking get:
kafka's little hyenas of society
on the meat of modern progress.

Yall are a bunch of hypocrites! You know damn well if you walked into a daycare with your baby & were told this is the person that would be caring for your newborn you wouldn't feel safe leaving your child with her all day yet you wanna sit here & act like everyone else is the problem for being concerned about the safety of a newborn left in her care. Unfortunately it is what it is, she can't control herself & to bring a child into this knowing her condition is just selfish.

The Voice of Common Wisdom Dictates:

 to bring a child into
this [redacted] is just
selfish.

And so:

 you [redacted]
were told
caring for your [redacted]
child
like everyone else is the problem

And every time, you want to scream
but you are tired
and you are sick
so you bite your tongue until it tastes of iron,
raging inside:

Yall are a bunch of hypocrites! You
damn
the person
all day yet you sit here & act
like the problem

I Can't Help But Be Famous – Devon Webb (she/her)

I need to stop posting on main
but I can't help but be famous
if I fuck them off well
thanks for the attention
being outspoken's just
part of the branding
& at least I'm speaking out
honey, I'm just practising
being a celebrity
my name is in demand
really, you demand things of me
like quiet & silence & politeness
fuck that
fuck your status quo bullshit
your anti-revolution
everyone the same kind of
pussy
I'm the kind of pussy that slaps
I'm the kind of pussy that gets itself off
I'm the kind of pussy that
doesn't need your feeble excuse for
coexistence like
being a coward could
somehow give me pleasure
let me redirect your unsolicited feedback
to the people who need it
look in the mirror
cos I'm no flat surface so
what the fuck do you think you're gonna get
from projecting
your distorted imagery doesn't quite
suit me
but I can't help being on your screens
you can't get enough of me
I break your boundaries
you box yourself in
you get defensive
I'm getting so big.

My Father Perches – Alex Carrigan (he/him)

> *—After Donna Vorreyer's "Heaven Only Knows"*

My father perches on my shoulder whenever I make a purchase or a decision.

His talons pierce through my pashmina whenever I stare at the price tag.

> The price tag tells me I have made enough wise choices to afford
>
> what it's offering, but my father pecks at my temple to jog my memory.

My memory reminds me of the nondescript cereal I bought, the thermos of

coffee I take to work instead of buying a Starbucks, the thrifted jeans I wear.

> I wear and eat what my father raised me on in the aerie he funded with
>
> odd jobs and excessive couponing, telling me this was the way the world is.

The world is open to academic scholarships and financial planning, and even now that

my father has tried to cast a wingspan over my eyes, I know what I can afford.

> I can afford something I know I can pay back with repeated usage, by sewing
>
> tears and removing stains with a bleach pen. He can go hunt mice instead.

Instead of feeling like he's flown freely, I remember that falcons are trained to return, so

my father still perches on my shoulder whenever I make a purchase or a decision.

internalized commercial interests – Melankalia Stambaugh (she/her)

field trips and questionnaires, poking and prodding, and pricking
stealing my plasma away to experiment and play
and come back with the knowledge that i
am healthy enough for some new poison
this one makes me heavier, this one might tint my skin yellow,
and leech my shit white as fine clay
...and if that happens, do give us a call...
so they can try to save my life from the life saving meds, sure
i had a ringside seat to bear witness to that and i didn't much enjoy it then
this one makes hair fall away like autumn leaves
and this one gives depression, like a
beautifully wrapped gift leaking carbon monoxide
so they ask about that, and i wonder
does my fucked up brain chemistry mean that
i can have the meds that make others despondent
or are we worried about layers upon layers of depression
like grasping for warmth with blanket after blanket until i smother to death
i confess, to enjoying the idea of life long depression
doubling as an antibody against further melancholy...
but i'm pretty sure that's not how that works
anyway.
human bodies are built wrong and, yes,
i would in fact like to speak to the manager
i've been on hold for years and i'm pretty sure they are never picking up
...your call is important to us, please stay on the line...
but, in the meantime,
we have a pill for aches, and a pill for sunshine,
and a pill for repressurizing your faulty blood flow,
a pill for panic—well it's not really *for* that
and it doesn't alleviate the anxiety, but we pretend
placebo effect, don'tcha know
all and sundry amount of pills for my mental state
...which only make you feel worse in the beginning, promise...
and i make believe that i don't think that's a lie
that i don't think it's all a lie
but the medicine is too big and the problem is unsolved
and i am tired, tired of trying things to see what sticks,
what helps a tiny bit, and what makes everything worse
i am exhausted from living in worse
all the while acknowledging that every time i type "live"

my phone changes it to "love", because it knows what's up
and how does my janky $5 phone,
the very same hunk of electronics that insists that "were" isn't a word,
that "we're" is what i mean every. single. time.
how does it know that a sense of connection, of acceptance,
of belonging, and community—that being heard is what i am most lacking
how does it know better what i need than all these medical professionals?

fall up
into
the sepia-toned sky
reverse the wind
and take me to the fires
let me watch the world actually burn
instead of seeing the apathetic response
of humanity smolder

A Pervasive, Long-Term Pattern – Jessi Carman (she/they)

i love you so much i hate your guts

and dream of mine spilling out

on the table, at dinner for everyone (for you) to see

so wet so open so warm so vulnerable

just as you asked

interpersonal relationship instability

i think about you all the time

and every sign from the universe is about you

ladybugs and dragonflies and 444 and 666

get out of my head

don't you have something better to do?

challenges in regulating emotional states to a healthy, stable baseline

citing my most destructive resources

as answers to the most irrational questions

bugs that aren't real and blood that's really probably water

the man in the hole in the ceiling that's too small to fit a man

who watches me shower

the neighbors aren't stalking me, not tonight

i'm not real anyway

stress-related paranoid ideation or severe dissociative symptoms

i'll tear it all to shreds

i'll burn everything down

reduce myself to ribbons

husk my soul out of my body like an ear of corn

painstakingly, peeling off the stringy bits

exhibit self-harming behaviours and engage in risky activities

please don't go

please please please

i can't do this without you

i don't know how to stay alive without you

don't you dare leave me

Frantic efforts to avoid real or imagined emotional abandonment

read at 3:42, fuck you and fuck your mom for pushing you out

or maybe it's all my fault

i'm the problem

i'm always the problem

it's always my fault

how could you do this to me?

extremes of idealization and devaluation.

it doesn't matter anyway

i lost the cause when i was a child

four years old, doomed

fulfillment only ever lasts an hour

Chronic feelings of emptiness.

it gets so hot in my chest

i think if i don't hit the car in front of me i'll die

but i've learned a little self control

and i don't want to hurt anyone (never)

so i just scream

intense anger that can be difficult to control

you were stolen from as a child, so you hate sharing

especially sharing me with myself

so i made a new skin for you

there are so many stations on this radio

and i can't tell which one tells the truth

safest to assume i must just be broken, guilty of something

A markedly disturbed sense of identity **and distorted** self-image.

it's easier without you

except that the longer i'm alone the deeper

into the dirt i burrow

cold earth the best comfort

down where i belong

Ariele Costantino (he/they)

I think i just accidentally accessed the secrets of the universe. I think my prayers at age 13 to whoever to make me omniscient worked. I think my mind cracked open that day and its been trying to put itself back together since. i think this is some odysseus, 'fatti non foste a viver come bruti' shit, or maybe some prometheus shit and the eagle slurps up my brain everyday and i dont even notice. Hey titan? Do you think it is worse to feel the agony every day or to not feel it at all? would you switch places with me if you could? is ignorance bliss?

Forgotten Music – Irina Tall (Novikova) (she/her)

With musical fingers a hundred
the only thread
And I'll cover my eyes with a dark bandage,
To weave the carpet of life...
And the white eagle will descend on me
And give him dark water to drink
Taking away the memory forever
In a series of rebirths
There, beyond that limit
I will only remember the words...

Victim Complex – Devon Webb (she/her)

I have a victim complex
not because I'm paranoid or imagined it but
because I have had it thrust upon me
by unkind souls
who consistently see a woman talking too much
too loudly
too much truth & they
want to shut her up
want the same old tune
same old stale misogyny
a pox on your name

a curse on your house where
you have tried to make a home
all those other thresholds
on fire

fuck you for trying to keep me quiet

I have had to dig myself out of
my own grave
too many times to count

at least I'm trying to communicate
around the dirt you heap in my mouth

I could choke
on the things you do to me
but I would rather survive

how does it feel
to see your ghosts

haunting the echo of your bad behaviour?

Awake and mostly sober – Rachael Ikins (she/her)

what the hell?
Dream vapor clings, fried egg reality.
I blink pie crust from my eyes. Conscious
and not high enough,
I fumble through the utensil drawer for a joint.
Finger joint, knuckle bone, fill the stock pot,
migraine on simmer.
Add mushrooms. Throw in an orphaned sock,
a lost earring.

Solo journey to technicolor awareness—it ain't all
it's cracked down to be,
just wrinkled meat, pignut hickory, bitter cache.
Smash it with a hammer, tweeze through pieces.

Anxiety nibbles a panic frayed around the edges,
thousand gerbil teeth squeak/squeak, squirrels gnawing
through your best defenses. A Xanax moment if ever there
was one, or how about a Klonopin, muffling fear, yes, panic,
feel needles' numb Neverland wrapped in a scarf
your grandmother crocheted before cataracts slingshot
her off the far cliff.

Three a.m. trots past, head, tail in the air, insomnia's golden
hour, German shepherds wearing teeshirts, all the tasks
you overlooked, pay bills, taxes, call a repair person for
the driveway, lay asphalt over all of it. Yeah, so thick
no obsession can crack it.

Awake and almost sober, startled by caffeine's
bright and shiny hit when, for a brief minute
your sinuses dilate blue-sky-sun, five o'clock
somewhere, wine erases first mistakes.

Dig a lint-haired gummy from
cement in your pocket
suck on it.
Go back to bed

where the lust you could
never have
slept between you
the whole decade, and now
when you lift your bowl to your lips,
you tongue tastes only dust.

BODY WITHOUT ORGANS
story DIA VAN GUNTEN
art BEPPI
IN THE OILY SOIL BENEATH THE OVERPASS, GUTTERED WITH GLASS, & LITTERED WITH PLASTIC, TWO WILD DOGS SCRAP OVER YOUR HEART WHICH YOU MEANT TO BURY VERY DEEP IN CASE YOU WANTED TO GO BACK FOR IT,
BUT YOU WERE DISTRACTED BY THE MATHEMATIC-RACKET COMING OFF THE RIVER, WHICH YOU NEVER LIKED NUMBERS WHEN YOU WERE ALIVE BUT NOW THEY'RE EVERYWHERE & YOU REALIZE YOU MUST'VE BEEN WRONG WHEN YOU TO MRS. WHAT'S-HER-NAME THAT NUMBERS HAD NOTHIN TO DO WITH NUTHIN,
BUT ALSO IT WAS THE SMARTEST THING YOU EVER SAID AS IT TURNS OUT, BECAUSE IT'S VERY HARD FOR NOTHING TO EXPRESS ITSELF WITHOUT NUMBERS PILED UP SO HIGH, A MOUNTAIN OF STINKING BODIES, & THEN THE RIGHT OR WRONG NUMBER COMES ALONG TO TIP THE WHOLE THING TO SHIT, SET IT AFIRE OR FEED IT TO YOU IN SOME WILD RITUAL OF CANNIBALISM
237
7
32
13
451
23
555
1968
& ALL YOU CAN DO IS STAND ON THE BRIDGE, & PLACE BETS ON WHICH DOG WILL WIN THE MEAT THAT USED TO BEAT INSIDE YOUR CHEST.
YOU CHEER AS THEY TEAR EACH OTHER TO SHREDS, & BLEED INTO THAT OILY SOIL
ALL WHILE THE TRUCKS GO
HUMP RUMP HUMP RUMP HUMP RUMP HUMP HUMP HUMP HUMP HUMP HUMP
HUMMITY HUMMITY HUMPTER-RUMP HUMHUM RUM RUMP RUMP PUNK PUNK PUNK
OVER THE METAL GRATING & THEN THE DOG WITH THE MISSING EAR EATS
& YOUR AORTA & SUDDENLY IT'S BACK IN YOUR CHEST.

THERE TIMES NOW YOU'VE THROWN YOUR GALLBLADDER INTO THE DETROIT RIVER, FLOATING IN A POP BOTTLE WITH A CAP THAT COULD'VE WON SOMEONE $10,000 IF THEY'D BOTHERED TO LOOK ON THE UNDERSIDE BEFORE TOSSING IT OUT THE WINDOW OF A SPEEDING CAR,
IT'S TOO LATE FOR YOU BECAUSE MONEY MEANS NOTHING TO THE DEAD SO YOU LIQUEFY YOURSELF FROM THE INSIDE & PEE YOUR GALLBLADDER INTO THE BOTTLE & YOU WHOOP AS IT'S SWEPT INTO THE CURRENT, FLOWING AWAY FROM YOU, BUT YOU FIND YOURSELF DOWNRIVER WITH A SCARRED GALLBLADDER, BECAUSE THE CAT IS ALIVE OR NOT, NO ONE IS SURE UNTIL THEY OPEN THE BOX, BUT THE CAT COMES BACK, VERY NEXT DAY, SO YOU STRAP YOUR GALLBLADDER TO A CEMENT BLOCK & YOU PRACTICALLY CUM WHEN IT SINKS INTO THE MUCK.
YOU'RE SURE HE'S A GONER BUT
THE CAT COMES BACK,
AS STINKING SLUDGE ON THE INSIDE OF A WASHED UP TIRE WHICH YOU ROLL DOWN THE ROAD FOR 3 MILES & THROW FROM A BRIDGE. BUT HE JUST CAN'T STAY AWAY, THE CAT KEEPS REMEMBERING ITSELF.
2
YOU'RE THE GUY NAILED TO THE ROCK, YOU GOT AN EAGLE THAT PECKS YOUR LIVER BUT SOON AS THE SUN RISES THE LIVER GROWS BACK FOR A NEW
PECK PECK PECK PECK WRECK WRECK PECK PECK PECK PUNK PUNK
OR MAYBE YOU'RE THE OTHER GUY WITH THE ROCK, ALL HE DOES IN LIFE IS PUSH THE ROCK UP A HILL BUT ALWAYS AT THE TOP, THAT ROCK ROLLS BACK, BOWLS HIM OVER, & HE'S FLAT LIKE WILE E. COYOTE ON THE ASPHALT BUT HE PEELS UP LIKE A COLORFORM & GETS BACK AT IT, ONE BREATH TO THE NEXT, TWO ROLLING BOULDERS.

THE LUNGS HAVE TO GO, THOSE PHLEGM FLECKED STONES, SO YOU TRAVEL BACK TO THE DESERTS OF PERSIA, BEFORE CHRIST, SINCE YOU'RE GETTING GOOD AT DEAD, & YOU MUST SURMISE THAT TIME IS ABSOLUTE UTTER NONSENSE, SO YOU WALK THE ANCIENT DESERT UNTIL YOU COME UPON THE HYENA, BUT BEFORE YOU CAN FEED THE ANIMAL YOUR LUNGS,
FIRST, YOU GOTTA EARN ITS TRUST BECAUSE THE BEAST IS SKITTISH & IT KNOWS ALL ABOUT MAGIC SO IT'S NOT FALLING FOR THE OLD LUNGS TRICK, IT'S NOT LOOKING TO BREATHE THE FUTURE, IT WOULD DIE OF SMOG RIGHT AWAY, OR WORSE IT WOULD BE INFECTED WITH A COMPUTER VIRUS, & YOU KNOW THIS BUT YOU DON'T CARE BECAUSE YOU'RE DESPERATE TO UNLOAD THESE LUNGS.
POOR HYENA HAS ENOUGH TROUBLE WITH THE GREEKS WHO WANNA SKIN HIM OR EAT HIS EYEBALLS OR TURN HIS ANUS INTO A POUCH FOR AMULETS BUT HE LIKES YOU, HYENA KNOWS A CORPSE WHEN HE SEES ONE SO HYENA COMES TO TRUST YA, ONCE YOU CLAW AT YOUR OWN DERMA & RIP AT YOUR RIBS & HAND FEED HIM THE MEAT, THOUGH YOU'VE BEEN WASTING, SO IT'S NOT MUCH, BUT IT'S THE THOUGHT THAT COUNTS.
THE FUTURE IS HARD ON THE HYENA, YOU KNEW IT WOULD BE, BUT YOU WEREN'T EXPECTING IT TO BE SO GORY, THE HYENA'S SEIZING & RATTLING, WITH SUCH VELOCITY, SUCH TECHNOLOGY, THAT HIS BRAIN MELTS & DRIPS OUT OF HIS NOTRILS LIKE HOT LAVA, & THE HYENA IS VOMITING BLOOD & MICRO PLASTICS & A VALYRIAN SWORD ENGRAVED WITH GLITTERING GLYPHS & THE 16th SEASON OF GILMORE GIRLS & THE HYENA HAS ALPHABET NOW SO IT SCREAMS IN 700 LANGUAGES:
SIRI, ORDER THE DISH SOAP! SIRI, SIRI, HOW COULD YOU DO THIS TO ME?! SIRI, WE DON'T CARE IF IT COMES IN RUSSIAN DOLL BOXES FROM AMAZON, OH GOD, SIRI, THAT FEELS GOOD, SIRI, SPIT IN MY MOUTH, SIT ON MY FACE, SIRI!
THE HYENA MOANS ECSTATICALLY, SWELLS, BULGES, LIKE A PYTHON & EXPLODES IN A GOOF OF OILY DUCKLINGS BORN OF MINED MOUNTAINS, WHO QUACK QUACK
IN ALGEBRAIC MADNESS, YOU GATHER BITS OF HYENA SKIN, EACH SHRED OF STRIPED FUR, AN AKASHIC RECORD, ONLY THE HYENA IS WHOLE AGAIN, BACK FOR MORE SUFFERING, ESOPHAGUS BLOCKED WITH A CROSSWAYS SHIP, A VIOLENT DEATH, ELECTRIC SPASMS.

YOU SCREAM:
YOUR WIFE SAYS:
SIR!
YOU BITCH! YOU FILTHY BITCH!.
I WARNED YOU, SANDRA
THIS WOMAN WITH THE DIAMOND HITS YOU AGAIN, AN ARCHING SIZZLE, SATANIC TECHNOLOGY, & NOW THESE DOG CATCHERS WITH THEIR NETS ARE CLOSING IN SO YOU FIGURE YOU MUST BE A FERAL DOG & YOU GO RABID, A FOAMING FOUNTAIN OF SNARLS, KICKING, LACES FLYING, THEN A SHOE, EXPOSING THAT ROTTEN FOOT, BIG TOE OOZING PUS & SWOLLEN UP LIKE A PEAR WHICH THE SMELL IS MORE POWERFUL THAN THE KICK SO YOU BREAK LOOSE & MAKE A RUN FOR IT BUT THAT PEAR TOE
POPS
& MAGGOTS CRAWL OUT.
YOU HOLD UP YOUR HANDS—
OKAY, OKAY, I'LL GO. I TOLD YOU I'D GO.
THEY STRAP YOU INTO THE VAN & LOCK YOU DOWN WHICH FEELS GOOD FOR A MOMENT, RESTFUL, & YOU SLIP AWAY TO THE LIBRARY WHICH HAS BOOKS BUT NOBODY OPENS THEM, THEY JUST KNEEL BEFORE THE FOUNTAIN & ASK FOR PERMISSION TO DRINK & THE TREES CONSULT THE MUSHROOMS & SAY
WE WILL ALLOW THIS BUT NOT EVERYONE CAN WITHSTAND IT, SOME WILL BE EXPLODING PYTHONS
BUT THE KNEELERS KNOW THIS BECAUSE THEY'VE ALREADY EXPLODED 7000 TIMES. THEY STILL CUP THEIR HANDS & DRINK THE WATER THAT FLOWS DOWN FROM THE MOUNTAIN OF BOOKS.
IN A BACK ROOM THERE'S AN OPIUM DEN FOR THE MORE ADVANCED, WHERE YOU PLUG IN DIRECT, BUT YOU'RE NOT READY FOR THAT, YOU'RE SNIFFING THE NOOSPHERE LIKE GLUE, YOUR WIFE'S PANTIES AS THE RAG, THE DOCTOR'S OFFICE IS SHAPED LIKE A PENIS BUT IT SMELLS LIKE PUSSY INSIDE, RIGHT AWAY YOU KNOW THE DEAL, YOU'RE NO DUM DUM, THEY KNEW YOU WERE COMING & THEY ARE PUMPING THIS SCENT INTO YOUR BRAIN AS A METHOD TO REEL YOU BACK TO YOURSELF, IT COULD'VE BEEN CHERRY PIE, FOR OTHERS IT MIGHT BE, OR VANILLA COOKIES OR SUNDAY LASAGNA OR THE SCENT OF YOUR GRANDMOTHER'S PERFUME. THERE'S CHERRY PIE TOO, ACTUALLY, FROZEN CRUST, DUMPED CAN OF CHERRIES.
4

IN THE OVEN

THE DOCTOR'S
ENTERS
TO THE NURSE,
CALL WOUND
CARE. FILE FOR
EMERGENCY
HOLD.

IT GETS VERY COMPLEX, A SACRED
GEOMETRY, ENDLESS REPETITION OF
CHERRIES & CRUST.
NOSTRILS FLARE WHEN HE
THE EXAM ROOM.

TO YOU, HELLO SANDRA,
WE CAN SEE YOU,
JUST SO YOU KNOW.

NO,
YOU CAN'T

YOU'D THINK DEATH
WOULD BE PEACEFUL
BUT IT'S WILD IN A WAY YOU COULD NEVER
IMAGINE, EVEN IF WHATS-HER-NAME HAD
ASSIGNED IT AS A SUBJECT, YEA, YOU COULD WRACK YOUR BRAIN & LET THE GOBLIN
LOOSE TO REALLY RANSACK THE WHOLE SCENARIO & YOU'D PROBABLY COME UP WITH
SOME WACKY SHIT IF YOU DUG DEEP INTO THE JUNGIAN STRATA, DOWN TO THE
HYPEROBJECTS & THE FORMATIVE WEIRDNESS & THE SUPPRESSED MEMORIES &
THE NIGHT TERRORS WHERE YOU LEFT YOUR BODY & FLOATED AROUND THE HOUSE
ONLY TO SEE THINGS NO CHILD SHOULD EVER SEE

5

& IT'S YOU
ALL GROWN UP WITH A LIGHT
BOX, A TV FOR YOUR LAP, & INSIDE, IT'S JUST PEOPLE RUTTING
LIKE ANIMALS IN SCREAMING, CREAMING FITS OF ORGIASTIC EXCESS, BUT THAT'S
NOT ENOUGH FOR YOU, IT'S ALWAYS MORE MORE MORE, SO YOU TYPE IN HORSE TO SEE
PEOPLE ON ALL FOURS WITH TAILS IN THEIR ASSES

& THEN
YOU TAKE IT FURTHER,
YOU GOTTA SEE A MAN GET REAMED BY A
HORSE FOR REAL, THE ONE WHO DIED BECAUSE
THE HORSE TORE HIM UP INSIDE, & THE FACT THAT
HE'S DEAD MAKES IT HOTTER BUT YOU'RE
ASHAMED WHEN YOUR WIFE CONFRONTS YOU SO
YOU LET HER CHALK IT UP TO CHILDHOOD TRAUMA
BECAUSE YOU'RE NOT THE KIND OF PERSON
WHO WANTS A MAN TO DIE FROM
INTERNAL HEMMORAGE JUST FOR
KICKS, YOU'RE THE DAMAGED SOUL WHO
WANTS TO SEE A MAN DIE IN A HUMAN
PUDDLE, BITS OF INTESTINES & BLOOD & STOOL, &
EVERYBODY IN THE WORLD KNOWS THAT THE MAN DID
THAT TO HIMSELF BECAUSE HIS DESIRE TO BE TAKEN
OVER BY SOMETHING LARGER THAN HIMSELF WAS
TURNING HIM INSIDE OUT LIKE THOSE RUBBERY
TUBE TOYS FROM CEDAR POINT, FLUID-FILLED SACS,
SLIPPERY BASTARDS, ALWAYS SLIPPING INSIDE OF THEMSELVES
& COMING OUT OF THEMSELVES & AS A CHILD YOU WON ONE FROM
THE CARNIVAL BARKER WHO COULDN'T GUESS YOUR AGE
BECAUSE YOU WERE STUNTED FROM ONLY EATING MASHED POTATOES & FRUIT LOOPS.

FOR A YEAR OR SO, AS A VERY SMALL, FERAL, HUNGRY, TREE CLIMBING KNEE SKINNED NUDIST-CLUB FOUNDER, POEM EATER, MASTURBATOR OF 8 YEARS, WELL YOU WERE WISE, BUT YOUR BRAIN WAS THE FIRST ORGAN YOU BURIED BECAUSE A GIRL IS NOT SUPPOSED TO BE SMART, SURE, SHE SHOULD GET GOOD GRADES & EARN SATIN RIBBONS & USE PUNCTUATION & DO HER LETTERS WITH CURLY CUES & YOU DO ALL OF THAT BUT, IN YOUR HEART, YOU KNOW THEY ARE WASTING YOUR TIME. THEY ARE MAKING YOU CUT & PASTE, THEY ARE SAYING IF YOU HAVE 67 HEARTS, HOW MANY DOGS WILL LOSE HOW MANY EARS OVER HOW MANY YEARS & HOW MANY TIMES WILL YOU BURY THE MUSHY ORGAN?
IT IS ENOUGH TO HOLD THAT ORGAN IN YOUR HAND, THAT PLASTIC TUBE THAT ATE ITSELF & SHIT ITSELF & SWALLOWED & SUCKED & FUCKED ITSELF & THAT'S ALL THE TOY DID BUT YOU COULDN'T PUT IT DOWN BECAUSE YOU KNEW IN YOU SOUL THAT IT WAS THE VERY HEART OF THE MATTER, THE SECRET OF THE UNIVERSE.
SANDRA, THIS INFECTION AFFECTS YOUR PARIETAL LOBE WHICH IS THE PHYSICAL EXPLANATION FOR YOUR EXPERIENCE AS DEAD BUT TRUST US, YOU ARE ALIVE, NOW, IT'S NOT UNCOMMON WHEN A PATIENT IS EXPERIENCING NEGATION FOR THEM TO IDENTIFY AS UNDEAD, AS A ZOMBIE OR A GHOST.
THE SECOND DOCTOR SMILED— WE'VE EVEN MET A FEW VAMPIRES.
HOW DO YOU IDENTIFY?
IN THE CORE OF YOUR BODY, THERE IS NOTHING. BUT THE THING NO ONE TELLS YOU ABOUT NOTHING IS HOW NOISY IT IS. THE SOUND IS SO MUCH THAT IT CAN ONLY BE SILENCE BECAUSE EVERYTHING IS NOTHING ONCE NUMBERS ARE UNTETHERED FROM DISCERNIBLE MATTER. THERE ARE SOUNDS YOU MISSED BEFORE, THAT RAVENOUS SLURPING, TREES PULLING SUNLIGHT INTO THEIR VEINS WITH THE SUCTION OF A BLACK HOLE WHO SLURPS A STAR INTO ITS MAW, UNWINDING IT FROM ITSELF IN ONE UNCURLING THREAD.
HMMP. SPAGHETTIFICATION, YES.
THE DOCTOR WHEELED CLOSER & LEANED IN TO WHISPER.
SANDRA? ARE YOU HEARING THE LOW LEVEL HISS OF PHOTOSYNTHESIS?
COURSING VEINS, SHIPPING LANES, FUNGAL PATHWAYS, NEURONAL NETWORKS, FLOWING BLOOD, FLOWING OIL, FLOWING DOLLARS..... LIGHT ..... LIFE ....
HUMP HUMP HUMP PUNKKITY PUNK PUNK.
6

I DESERVE TO BE ANGRY I JUST WANT TO BE MORE – arushi (aera) rege (they/them)

I WANT MORE THAN JUST HELLOS & I WANT TO BE ALIVE & I WANT TO BE HAPPY & I WANT EVERYTHING TO BE MINE & I WANT SALT ON MY BUTTERED BREAD & I WANT SOCIETY TO GIVE ME WHAT IT OWES ME & I WANT TO BE SEEN AS GIRLBOY NOT JUST GIRLFRIEND & I WANT TO STOP BEING CALLED SOMEONE'S BITCH & I WANT TO STOP HAVING GIRLFRIEND ATTACHED TO MY NAME LIKE A CURSE LIKE A PROMISE LIKE A REDUCTION OF THE SELF & I WANT EVERYONE TO FEAR ME & I WANT EVERYONE TO LOVE ME & I WANT EVERYTHING ALL THE TIME & I WANT TO BE SORRY & I WANT TO STOP BEING SORRY & I WANT TO REMEMBER THAT HUNGER IS ANOTHER WORD FOR DESIRE IS ANOTHER WORD FOR GREED IS ANOTHER WORD FOR LOVE & I WANT TO NEVER GO TO THE ER AGAIN & I WANT TO GO TO SLEEP FOREVER EVEN IF IT'S A METAPHOR FOR DEATH & I WANT MY BOYFRIEND TO STOP JOKING ABOUT BREAKING UP & I WANT TO STOP HAVING PANIC ATTACKS AFTER SPEECH & DEBATE COMPETITIONS & I WANT TO BREAK EVERYONE WHO TOLD ME THEY HATED ME & I WANT TO KILL EVERYTHING THAT DARES ANGER ME & I WANT TO BE ANGRY & I WANT TO QUIT BEING THIS WAY & I WANT EVERYTHING THAT HAS EVER ANGERED ME TO GO AWAY & I WANT TO HAUNT MY BODY & I WANT MY BODY TO STOP HAUNTING ME & I WANT TO BE ALONE OR WITH EVERYONE OR WITH ONE SPECIFIC PERSON FOREVER & I WANT TO BE TWO EXIT WOUNDS WITH NO POINT OF ENTRY FOR MY RAGE GREED HURT LOVE & I WANT TO PRETEND THAT PYRRHIC VICTORS ARE VICTORS NONETHELESS & I WANT TO BE ABLE TO TELL YOU THAT I'M SORRY & I WANT MY BOYFRIEND TO STOP LOOKING AT ME WITH ONLY LOVE IN HIS EYES I DESERVE TO BE HATED I DESERVE WORSE I DESERVE TO BE DESIRED WANTED EVERYTHING & I WANT TO PASS ALL MY CLASSES & I WANT TO BE ANGRY & I WANT EVERY POEM TO STOP READING LIKE A METAPHOR FOR LOVE OR DESIRE OR GREED JUST ONCE & I WANT TO START WRITING ABOUT SHIT THAT REALLY MATTERS EXCEPT I'M NOT SURE ANYTHING I WRITE HAS MEANING ANYMORE & I WANT TO WRITE ABOUT SOMETHING OTHER THAN RAW DESIRE TWIN KISSED LIPS SHADE COPENHAGEN & I WANT TO BE SOMEONE GREATER THAN MYSELF LIVE WITHOUT THE DESTRUCTION OF MY BODYSELF & I WANT TO BE MORE THAN JUST A LONELY LITTLE POET

The Price – William Roberds King (he/him)

Some things belong together, paired like

salt and pepper shakers

bookends

adultery and literary fiction

film students and cigarettes

and according to our mother

my brother and I.

we had to stay together, we were

a matching set

she said. We weren't the same height,

my brother and I,

he was thinner than I.
His hair is lighter than mine
before mine curled, people believed

we were twins

He got a Dr. Attwood's Diagnosis™
of Autism. I was told to be the
the normal one. Our mother said we

both

can't be

Autistic.

In her mercenary love, Mother only
cared so long there was a

profit. Custody

has its perks after all. And who cares
about the

condition of merchandise

that depreciates when

we come of age?

Off The List – Zo Copeland (they/them)

Whitecoat supremacy
You can't pin me down
If you're not going to help me
You're helping me drown

Did you hear the news?
I died tonight
With no-one beside me
And no will to fight

You left me so long
That I ceased to exist
I jumped off the top of
...your waiting list

natural (re)born entertainer – jp thorn (he/they/any)

preschool—it's 1993
teachers offer donuts before class
if i bat my eyelashes for them,
sprawled dark desert palms
awning over gray beta fish eyes;

a paid performer before
i can parse an idea of capitalism,
arced towards patriarchal needs
new jester of the court,
nobility as licensed fool
my function reduced to
single-sourced entertainment &
still a cultural pillar,
2/52 in every deck.

this burden will press
permanence
into agnate boulders
stored in your breast pocket
or shelved in your mind when
your life depends on
rallying men with asinine whimsy,
they're so often one in the same

though this is how some imps
learned to *keep up the act*
is how to stay alive,
torn birth ticket admits one
to the upper crust,
fawn in the grass
shivers itself to pieces nightly
as odious power games
hobble onward,
last names collages of
intermixology & insider trading.

but fools?
we *are* this job, the declaration
expected to be proud,

having danced upstream
post-uterine gates,
trajectory fixed as
saturday fight nights,
marbled rubber chimera balls
bounced off ornate ceilings,
through this life into the next
infinitely grandiose hall

Well who's fault is it then?
It's all about lifestyle and choices of what we put in our bodies.
For example Obesity causes so many chronic illnesses and co-morbidities, yet people don't stop eating crap food. It's only when they get a chronic illness resulting from obesity that they start moaning. Solution stop shovelling food into your mouths, get active and change your life style. That is the most stupid statement I have read. (Those born with genetic driven illness are not included in my statement before anyone starts ranting).

1

Well who's fault[15] is it then? It's all about lifestyle and choices[16] of what we put in our bodies.[17] For example Obesity[18] causes so many chronic illnesses and co-morbidities[19], yet people don't stop eating crap[20] food. It's only when they get a chronic illness resulting from obesity that they start moaning[21]. Solution stop shovelling food[22] into your mouths, get active[23] and change your life[24] style. That is the most stupid statement I have read.[25] (Those born with genetic driven illnesses are not included in my statement[26] before anyone starts ranting[27]).

---

[15] Disability is wrong. It's important to place the blame somewhere. Ideally, place the blame on the individual unable to bootstrap their way through any adversity; let's not get unhinged and find fault in the medical system or the legal system or any other kind of larger problem with our society. Our society is great. How dare you.

[16] Choices are the best way to find fault with a person and their body. It's not 'politically correct' anymore to say that disability is bad, but saying the disabled person's *choices* were / are / always will be bad is a fine consolation prize.

[17] Every disabled person reading this likely knows where this is going.

[18] Capitalized like a god, because we worship at the altar of the ugly medical word for ugly fatness that we cannot tolerate, but it gives us cause to find fault and name it, shame it, save it in our back pocket for a rainy day.

[19] What is the rate of co-morbidities with non-obesity? What is the medical term for someone who isn't obese?

[20] Perhaps this helpful commenter just wants there to be a universal program for access to free, healthy food.

[21] A Moan: "a low, mournful cry of pain, sorrow or pleasure" (per Wiktionary). Basically any of the major conditions of being human. To be in pain causes cries of pain; this is the great revelation? Or perhaps that we are given grief like a gift wrapped in old newspaper obituaries. Or pleasure, because sometimes we accidentally happen upon that, too.

[22] Now the solution: stop eating. Period. Not just crap food. Food. Any. Stop. Your survival is offensive.

[23] A wheelchair is no excuse. A cane is no excuse. Pain is no excuse. Energy is no excuse. (Translation: If I must be miserable, you don't get out of the misery!)

[24] Your whole life, really. Acting like it's a 'lifestyle' issue is just a courtesy.

[25] To be fair, this statement was still in the process of being written when this claim was made.

[26] Such generosity!

[27] Too late.

> This is the classic emotional manipulation and blackmail that cults often use. There are many new and rigorous peer reviewed empirical studies demonstrating the negative outcomes, risks and harm of hormones/surgeries for kids/youth, including HIGHER risk of suicide by 5 years past surgery. Not to mention research showing that "watchful waiting" results in close to 90% of kids growing out of gender dysphoria by adulthood while 80% end up being homosexual. Why turn gay and vulnerable kids into suicidal lifelong medical patients when support, counselling and helping them to accept their natural healthy body results in positive outcomes in nearly 90% of the case?

Students' comments were particularly elaborative compared to those of adults in the LGBTQ+ You study, and their discussion of euphoria likely benefitted from the enhanced clarity emotion brings youth [29]. Past research emphasises that dysphoria models overlook nonbinary and transmasculine people's experiences [30]; these data show euphorias as especially useful for identifying and understanding such youths' experiences. The study showed pedagogies endorsing diversity and students' requested names/pronouns supported in anti-suicide data [1, 31, 32], also support students' Category Validation euphorias. Teachers could be LGBTQ+ youth euphoria builders or blockers, refecting research linking teacher rejection to increased wellbeing risks [14, 33, 34].[28]

In particular, social support from parents... was associated with reduced risk for lifetime suicide attempts.[29]

---

[28] Jones, Tiffany. *Euphorias in Gender, Sex and Sexuality Variations: Positive Experiences*. Palgrave MacMillain, 2023.
[29] Mustanski, Brian and Richard T. Liu. "A Longitudinal Study of Predictors of Suicide Attempts Among Lesbian, Gay, Bisexual, and Transgender Youth. *Archives of Sexual Behavior*, vol. 42, no. 3, 2013, pp. 437-448.

is bullshit. No kid is committing
suicide because of a pronoun.
You guys assume that but it's
deeper than that. They're all
mentally ill, maybe focus on
that and get over yourselves. So
delusional with your ideologies
so far up your arse.

This finding was very much congruent with Hatzenbuehler's (2009) contention that (1) LGBT individuals experience more stressors in large part because of stigma relating to their sexual orientation; (2) this greater experience of stressors in turn increases distress and emotion dysregulation; and (3) these manifestations of distress confer risk for psychopathology (e.g., suicidality). Moreover, family support may exert its promotive effect indirectly by reducing hopelessness and MDD symptoms. Finally, these proximal risk factors may also serve as a mediational pathway underlying the relation between CD symptoms and suicide attempts. This pattern of mediation suggests that preventing victimization of LGBT youth could decrease suicide attempts by decreasing hopelessness and depression. Similarly, family-based interventions that increase support could reduce hopelessness and depression symptoms, thereby reducing the likelihood of a suicide attempt.[30]

Let's not forget to mention ...
appearances. I'd NEVER hire that thing
to represent my company.

In determining the gender of each person we encounter and in present genders to others, we rely extensively on these gender displays. Our bodies and their adornments provide us with "texts" for reading a person's gender (Bordo 1993).[31]

---

[30] Mustanski, Brian and Richard T. Liu. "A Longitudinal Study of Predictors of Suicide Attempts Among Lesbian, Gay, Bisexual, and Transgender Youth. *Archives of Sexual Behavior*, vol. 42, no. 3, 2013, pp. 437-448.
[31] Lucal, Betsy. "What It Means to Be Gendered Me: Life on the Boundaries of a Dichotomous Gender System." *Gender and Society*, vol. 13, no. 6, 1999, pp. 781-797.

What's funny is all these things are
white, way overweight females, who
also die their hair 4 different colors,
and have extreme facial piercings and
other crap, like this one shaving her
eyebrows. Because they are screaming
for attention, because otherwise they
don't. Pathetic.

[Erving] Goffman rejected the idea that gender is a corollary of biological sex. Instead, he aimed to interrogate how gender is communicatively constructed, displayed and more appositely, a 'schedule for presenting' pictures of masculinity and femininity. Goffman's work on gender display has inspired contemporary understandings of gender as a routine accomplishment embedded in everyday interaction achieved through a process of 'doing' in so far as there is no pre-existing being behind the act (West and Zimmerman, 1987).[32]

They can join the circus, for that's
where these people belong.

Evil Cave Boy, a twenty-seven-year-old performance artist, echoes these sentiments: "Sometimes I'm very masculine, sometimes very feminine depending on my situation; I go back and forth all the time." Evil Cave Boy elaborates her gender position further by comparing herself to "a freak, a muse, a joker, a clown."[33]

---

[32] Baker, Stephanie Alice and Michael James Walsh. "'Good Morning Fitfam': Top posts, hashtags and gender display on Instagram." *New Media & Society,* vol. 20, no. 12, 2018, pp. 4553-4570.
[33] Halberstam, Jack. *Female Masculinity.* Duke University Press, 1998.

So in other words you're spoiled brat,
with severe mental issues that were
never treated and now the rest of
the world has to suffer because your
mother failed you? Is that accurate?
By the way nobody takes you serious
anyway because you look like you
tripped and fell face first into a tackle
box

Some psychological theorists, in an attempt to explain homosexuality's deviant nature, promoted the notions that same-sex attractions might be caused by the ineffective resolution of a childhood complex or by the skewed relational patterns of parents, such as an overbearing mother and a weak or distant father causing a man to be gay. The goal of analysis was to resolve these issues and return to a "normal" heterosexual life.[34]

Mental Illness masquerading as
alternative gender choices.

Things are the way they are by virtue of the fact that men are men and women are women-a division perceived to be natural and rooted in biology, producing in turn profound psycho- logical, behavioral, and social consequences. The structural arrangements of a society are presumed to be responsive to these differences.[35]

We are ALL sick and tired of all the
Mental illness running rampant
nowadays

LGBT activists have argued that individual feelings, especially those related to shame, are often a product of homophobic social structures rather than simply personal issues. Until the 1970s, the American Psychiatric

---

[34] Albert, Guy. "Fix Me Please: I'm Gay!" *Headcase: LGBTQ Writers and Artists on Mental Health and Wellness*, edited by Stephanie Schroeder and Teresa Theophano, Oxford University Press, 2019, pp. 169-177.
[35] West, Candace and Don H. Zimmerman. "Doing Gender." *Gender and Society*, vol. 1, no. 2, 1987, pp. 125-151.

Association's Diagnostic and Statistical Manual of Mental Disorders (DSM) listed homosexuality as a mental disorder. By targeting homophobic bias in the mental health professions, activists challenged the stigmatization of LGBT people and argued for recognition of empirical research demonstrating that homosexuality was a normal sexual variation. Despite success in removing homosexuality from the DSM in 1973, persistent cultural perceptions of homosexuality as deviant, shameful, or immoral create conditions that may encourage individuals to hide or feel shame about their desires, practices, and identities and thus to remain closeted. As the example of the DSM suggests, institutional closets result from practices that privilege heteronormativity and pathologize or prohibit LGBT desires, identities, and sexual expression. Politically, laws prohibiting same-sex marriage and criminalizing sodomy created conditions of secrecy and danger. The 1986 U.S. Supreme Court decision in Bowers v. Hardwick, which upheld the constitutionality of a Georgia sodomy statute, demonstrated that LGBT people could not claim a fundamental right to consensual sexual activity, even in the privacy of their homes.[36]

I'm not dismayed by the number of trans people seen in those circles (higher than average); I'm dismayed by the kind of trans person. I'm talking the typical spergy AGP named something like Luna or Artemis. The kind who won't shut the fuck up about the drugs they take or sperg about "periods."

What sucks has been my effort to find normie hobbies. Being hypomasculine, I never quite fit in, I still don't. This is ironically I guess sort of a "transition" in and of itself.

The queer future is not on the screen, but in the critical engagement, in the critical resistance, and in the queer demand and queer refusal to frame our lives with conventional narratives and straight timelines. Queer rhetoric can continue the work of teaching us to read more queerly, to move through the world more queerly. Queer rhetorical work must always understand that normativity will always have the home court advantage, while queers are always lingering in anticipation of their not-yet home. Normativity will always do that seductive work of appealing to the familiar, the sensible, the comfortable, the "good queer," and arguing something is (probably) queer enough. This demands we fight to engage a text with persistent reflexivity, understanding any comforts and concessions we may find in those normative grammars are likely being bridged at the expense and exclusion of another—those gorgeously defiant "bad queers" who continue to

---

[36] Raimondo, Meredith. "Closet." *Encyclopedia of Lesbian, Gay, Bisexual, and Transgender History in America,* edited by Marc Stein, Charles Scribner's Sons, vol. 1, 2004, pp. 227-231.

make trouble, not fit in, resist the safe bridging into mainstream stories, and remain aliens to a future that is not, presently, queer enough.[37]

sperg

Verb

(intransitive, slang, derogatory) To have a tantrum or fit of rage.

    Synonym: spaz

(intransitive, slang, derogatory, sometimes reclaimed) To ramble in excessive detail, as someone with Asperger's syndrome would stereotypically do.[38]

> I think you're spot on, and it's fucked because these freaks are utterly destroying people's perception and treatment of genuine transgender women, who have it rough enough as it is. They have taken over trans communities to the point where *you'll get banned for saying that you need gender dysphoria to be trans.* It's like with autism; the more that completely normal people declare themselves autistic, the less likely it is that the genuinely autistic will receive any kind of understanding or acceptance or support.

Such constant and invasive surveillance of non-visibly disabled bodies is the result of a convergence of complicated cultural discourses regarding independence, fraud, malingering, and entitlement; the form it takes almost always involves a perceived discontinuity between appearance, behavior, and identity.[39]

---

[37] Goltz, Dustin Bradley. "Rhetorics of Gay Future and Queer Futurity: Strategies of Disruption." *The Routledge Handbook of Queer Rhetoric,* edited by Jacqueline Rhodes and Jonathan Alexander, Routldge, 2022, pp. 413-420.

[38] https://en.wiktionary.org/wiki/sperg

[39] Samuels, Ellen. "MY BODY, MY CLOSET: Invisible Disability and the Limits of Coming-Out Discourse." *GLQ,* vol. 9, no. 1-2, 2003, pp.233-255.

To your second question, I think a lot of trans
people transition because they think it's easier to
be a woman if they're not traditionally masculine.
We can either change social norms which would
be way difficult to accept those types and make
them socially/romantically viable/desirable or
help them be more masculine. All of the MtFs
I've known were similar to me personality wise
somehow, traits like being on the spectrum,
introverted, a loner, low self esteem and
confidence etc. They think it's a magic pill but it
really isn't

For much of my life, my masculinity has been rendered shameful by public responses to my gender ambiguity.[40]

Transsexuals, and later transgenders, were disparaged because some were "passing" as straight through embrasure of stereotypes of gendered behavior, i.e., effeminacy for MTFs and hyper-masculinity for FTMs, and embrasure of heterosexual practices and privilege by identifying their same-sex practices as heterosexuality, thus rejecting homosexual identity. They were also looked down upon because they violated cultural norms of sexual behavior through gender ambiguity, visible androgyny and genderqueerness, thus violating the accommodationist idea that they are "just like you."[41]

It's a virus we should find vaccine for
them

At all scales of social life, from the individual to the nation and beyond, the rhetoric of disease and contagion draws attention to the porosity and persistent vulnerability of borders. In the case of transphobic discourse directed at AFAB trans people, the border anxiety in question is that which distinguishes men from women. In what follows, I chart out the four components of virality: the virus, the environment, the hosts, and time (Seas 55).[42]

---

[40] Halberstam, Jack. *Female Masculinity.* Duke University Press, 1998.

[41] Weiss, Jillian Todd. "GL vs. BT: The Archaeology of Biphobia and Transphobia Within the U.S. Gay and Lesbian Community." *Journal of Bisexuality,* vol. 3, no. 3-4, 2003, pp. 25-55.

[42] Randall, Liam. "Irreversible Damage: Trans Masculine Affectability and the White Family." *The Routledge Handbook of Queer Rhetoric,* edited by Jacqueline Rhodes and Jonathan Alexander, Routledge, 2022.

What a complete mess of a human.
We need to fund and bring back insane
asylums. This would create jobs
and help with lunatics like this and
homeless.

The medicalization of the sexually peculiar was both the effect and the instrument of this. Imbedded in bodies, becoming deeply characteristic of individuals, the oddities of sex relied on a technology of health and pathology. And conversely, since sexuality was a medical and medicalizable object, one had to try and detect it-as a lesion, a dysfunction, or a symptom-in the depths of the organism, or on the surface of the skin, or among all the signs of behavior.[43]

Euthanasia is prudent at this juncture
of societal collapse. We've hit the end,
fellow Romans.

Inferior people could not be allowed into the United States. This obviously included Africans and Asians, who had been barred from entry by a series of immigration laws enacted over the past two decades, as had lunatics, disabled people, people with any of a list of diseases, and those who could not afford to pay the head tax. In 1917, for overtly eugenic reasons, Congress barred people who were feebleminded, morally degenerate, or sexually suspect as well. But they were not satisfied.[44]

Both the lone lunatic and the crazed collective stage a desire that I have called queer utopia.[45]

---

[43] Foucault, Michel. *The History of Sexuality: Volume 1*. Translated by Robert Hurley, Pantheon Books, 1978.
[44] McWhorter, Ladelle. "Enemy of the Species." *Queer Ecologies,* edited by Catriona Mortimer-Sandilands and Bruce Erickson, Indiana University Press, 2010.
[45] Munoz, Jose Esteban. *Cruising Utopia: The Then and There of Queer Futurity.* NYU Press, 2009.

and I bu
of the r

burning

your rain
embrace me
burning

I burn
as your rain
embrace me

embraced
burning
rain

we embrace
and I burn
of the rain

embraced
burning
rain

I burn
as your rain
embrace me

embraced
burning
rain

your rain
embrace me
burning

embraced
burning
rain

I burn
as your rain
embrace me

we embrace
and I burn
of the rain

embraced
burning

your rain

your burning

embrace me

burning

we em

and I b

of the

embraced
burning
rain

escaping oppression to oppress – john compton (he/him)

dear zionists,
will you celebrate chanukah
by using eight palestinian people
as candles: will you light your menorah
with imprisoned civilians—
use their hair as wicks?
their membrane as wax?
will you believe each body you desecrate
represents a light
to cancel out your darkness?
while their skin burns
& their blood boils—
will you blame their screaming
for your ruined holiday?

Best Friends Forever – Alexandra Weiss (he/they)

You'd never guess if you met me now, but, before I died, I felt completely and utterly alone. It sounds impossible to be lonely in a city as crowded as Los Angeles. But before she appeared, senior year seemed like it would be just as lonely as the rest of high school. It's not from lack of trying that I don't really fit in here. Being gray^2, I don't have much to say about hookups and first dates. And when the conversation shifts to things I love, like bad movies or good books, my anxiety spikes and I just can't make the words come out. Especially with people staring, which people love to do at the only clocky person in the room. Always somehow invisible and way-too-visible. Therapy hasn't helped much, not yet anyways. Nor does being short and curvy. It's a lot harder to be confident when you know everyone sees the ghosts of your past in your face, even when 6 months of T have started to work their magic. I think I'm just better online.

At lunch, I sit at the edge of the table, smiling and laughing with the kids from English class, trying to pretend that I'm somebody else. Sometimes I go to parties, but once couples start to form and splinter off, I get bored and lonely and feel out of place. I'm a good acquaintance though: always happy to listen, if you don't mind nervous energy and use my true name. As for deep friendships, the queerplatonic kind, well...mom always says you don't really "meet your people" until college or your thirties or something. I'd been holding out hope that turning eighteen would somehow shift things, make it easier. I've been officially an adult for nearly a year, since just after last Halloween. Still stuck here for one more birthday and six months beyond, but then I'll be going out into the world, trying to make it as a writer, as a person, with no more answers and no less nervousness than I had last summer. Terrifying. I slog through my social anxiety in the hopes that I'll be able to connect to someone, anyone, instead of just wasting time hoping the future will be better. But I feel really invisible at PS #315. Doubly so because I'm still too scared to go to the men's bathroom here, or to take off my oversize hoodie, or to show emotion. I feel like a ghost. Or I did until they walked through the door.

The new kid is really quiet. It's as if the crepe velvet of their long dark skirt muffles the usual murmur that accompanies a new student like the heavy hush of theater curtains. She doesn't say a word, only smiles as Mr. Daniels points her to her seat. I'm relieved not to be the only quiet one in Mr. Daniels' history class anymore. It got lonely at the back of the classroom, *The Master and Margarita* stuffed awkwardly into the open AP textbook. Reading to make the day go by faster like I have somewhere better to be (I don't). Now here's this quiet person, slipping into the empty desk next to mine, left corner, last row. Her dark, curly hair covers one brown eye and cascades down a purple and black striped shirt, coming to a rest by her elbows. Their eye meets mine. I look down at my hands, black nails scuffed and peeling, skin still smudged with the remains of last night's charcoal. I'm the only high school student in the night session of figure drawing at the local art center. 7:30-10:30 Tuesdays and Thursdays. I don't feel out of place in the quiet shadows of the studio, or the deserted streets biking home after class. At art class, nobody looks at me with the weight of years of puberty and memories of long hair I hated and dresses I had used to overcompensate. They barely register me at all, just another guy at his easel, each of us focused on the little worlds of our own sketches. And by the time I leave, charcoal-covered hands holding a paper cup of mint tea for warmth, there's nobody around. People go to bed early in my neighborhood, even if our desert city never shuts down. My classmates disperse to their cars, drive home to late family dinners or leftovers, until it's just me and coyotes and scorpions. I feel so free under cover of darkness. Free to be the pretty boy in my heart. Free to feel the wind brush past my ears, the butterflies in my chest that accompany reminders of my haircut. I just wish it weren't so lonely under the palm trees and pines.

Squinting through the edge of my glasses I look back in her direction, but she's facing away from me now, eyeing the bookshelf. Standard fare. I watch her hands, fidgeting in her lap, the only part of her that seems to move. They're bony, olive and smooth. They look fun to draw. Hands are always a challenge, so many bony landmarks and so familiar that viewers without much anatomical knowledge can easily tell when you've fucked them up. But I love drawing hands, because they're so alive, full of gesture and fluid movement. As if on cue, her hands dart up to the shelf, pulling down the battered copy of *Dracula* that nobody seems to have noticed I scribbled in. Blushing, I wonder if she'll read my notes, if she'll judge me for using a sparkly green pen or writing in a borrowed book, or for writing weird messages to nobody in the first place. Or maybe they'll write something back.

Curtaining her desk with hair I now notice has dark green highlights, she starts to read. I smile at the thought that we might have more in common than books and silence. She's wearing an awful lot of purple and green for a person who isn't aro-ace. Fuck. Time to try and talk myself into enough confidence to say hi after class. Reaching down to my patched and duct-taped black backpack I unzip the middle pocket and start fishing for the rusty old Altoids tin full of anxiety meds. But just as my hand hits metal, it freezes. Eyes bore into the side of my head. I try to turn, but can't. I try to cough, nothing. Am I even breathing? Suddenly the medicine isn't prophylactic anymore. But this is more than my normal panic. Is this what dying feels like? Stars swarm my field of vision, blurring the distant blackboard. Then, just as suddenly, my heart restarts and I hear blood rush past my ears. I get up, flustered, knocking over both my books in the process and run for the door, the hallway, the safety of the single user bathroom. Mr. Daniels' calls out "Do you have a hall pass, Leona?" Even when I'm panicked, the slap of my deadname stings like a pulled stitch. Gritting teeth I blurt out "asthma attack!" before staggering to the door. This doesn't really feel like my usual asthma attacks, but I don't know what else it could be. Plus, I haven't had one since starting HRT, so maybe asthma is just one of those things that works differently on T, like crying? My heart is racing and my lungs burn. The door shuts behind me, the hallway deserted. Shoving my inhaler and spacer together I puff medicine that only makes me jumpier, and head to the single user bathroom, a safe place to hide behind its familiar, peeling gray door. Grabbing the handle, I'm ready for the relief of a private moment to slow my pulse and catch my breath when the door opens, almost hitting me in the nose and I'm face to face, or more accurately, face to neck with her. She's tall. I always forget that at 5', I'm pretty short, even for a trans guy. I jump back, reflexively startled by her presence. How'd she beat me here? I could have sworn I saw her at her desk through the closing classroom door.

None of that matters. She's staring me in the eyes and I can't look away. I shuffle past her, slowly turning to walk backwards into the open door because this eye contact is really, weirdly, nice, instead of the usual terrifying, and I don't want to break it. I try to smile, she smirks back, and then the bell rings, breaking the spell. Swallowing as much of my anxiety as I can I say "hi."

"I'm Leo, he/they" I'm sweating, purple curls sticking to the back of my neck. But still calmer than usual, still able to speak.

"Hyacinth, she/they" That's a pretty name. Like the poet.

"You're new here, right?" What is happening to me?

"Yeah. Good thing I'm in your class." She smiles down at me, eyes dark and entrancing.

They're so pretty. What does she mean by "good thing"?

"What do you mean-" I feel shyness come rushing back, flicking my green eyes to the linoleum beneath our feet, my scuffed black platform boots and her oxblood creepers.

"Let's just say that I think you and I are going to be great friends." She smiles, placing a cold hand on my shoulder. I'd normally shiver, flinching at the unexpected contact. But somehow, I think she's right. Looking up at her, kind of confused but drawn to her as the cool new kid who's also non-binary, who also seems to also be a mall goth literature dork, who seems to be able to see through my skittish exterior, who seems interested in me back, I ask a question I've been too scared to ask since middle school.

"Would you maybe wanna come over after school?" Silence.

"I saw you...uh...reading in class-not that I was staring or anything!! But I mean I like to read, too and maybe, we could, you know, read together?" Their smile widens, their hand tightens on my shoulder, pinpricks of pain dotting where long black nails made little dents in my sweater. Leaning down to whisper in my ear, she says "Eight o clock. Come to my place, though. I'm still unpacking and could use your input on decorating." Then, address scrawled on my right wrist in blood-red ink, they're gone in a flutter of green and black curls, flowing skirt and echoing laughter.

The bell rings again and I make my way to biology class. Copying diagrams of mitosis and cellular respiration, I smell iron. There's something wet oozing from the points where her fingertips met my skin. Blushing, again. Her nails made me bleed! Why does that make me feel like smiling? My shoulder throbs throughout the rest of class, dully aching through lecture after lecture, pulsating with the promise of companionship, someone to swap books with, have inside jokes with, make playlists with, fall asleep curled up next to after an all-night movie marathon. I've been desperate, yearning for a friendship where I can actually be myself, the chance to be alone together with somebody who doesn't need me to be somebody else.

The rest of the day passes in a haze of daydreams and wishful thinking. It's intoxicating, dizzying to let myself imagine. Squishy. I recognize this feeling from all the classic representations, Sherlock and Watson, Cristina and Meredith Grey. But the closest thing I've felt to this electricity was the first time I stuck testosterone into my thigh. The realization that I can be any version of Leo Nepenthes I want. Maybe we could dress up together for Halloween, even if the rest of this town seems to stop celebrating by fourteen, let alone adulthood. Maybe we could stay out all night at the beach, watching waves crash into cold sand filled with nocturnal ocean life, sand crabs, fluorescent ctenophores swimming in reflected starlight.

I could have sworn I read the address she gave me right. I followed my phone's directions and when that got me nowhere strictly residential, I even tried switching search engines, retracing my steps before pedaling back up the big hill on the west side of town. But no, it's seven fifty five and here I am standing under the gates to Violet Cemetery. I'm crushed. Is it a prank? Is she even gonna show? Maybe any second now she'll jump out from behind a weeping willow, phone camera flash in my face, laughing. I turn, looking towards the parking lot, but my bike is just as isolated as it was ten minutes ago. But when I turn back around, there she is, her face inches from mine, sitting on the top of a gravestone covered in moss and lichen. She looks different out from under public school fluorescents. For starters, their fishnets don't pass dress code.

She's wearing black matte lipstick and carrying a picnic basket. They gesture through the wrought iron gate into the gloaming.

"Make yourself at home." Weaving between headstones and mausoleums, occasionally adorned with wilting flowers, she comes to a stop outside a small, low crypt, stone worn with age, name long lost to wind, rain, and time. I follow her, confused but ultimately just happy my fears were ungrounded.

"Welcome to my safe haven," they smile, opening the basket. She pulls out a thick black fleece blanket, a zippo, and a handful of small orange candles. Lighting the candles before returning to the basket, her eyes shine in their small flames as she retrieves two chipped mugs, a thermos, and a book that definitely isn't in our school library.

"Holy crap. That's my chapbook!" They've read my writing? How did they find it?

"I've been lonely too." she says as if that's answer enough, and it is, somehow. She breaks eye contact first, turning to watch the pines as she passes me a goblet and a second book.

"This one's mine."

"Wait. You're Hyacinth Sycamore?" she nods, her quizzical look shifting to amused understanding as I scramble in my backpack, pulling out my copy of her collection, dog eared with love. They laugh, deep music echoing through darkening cemetery.

"I had no idea you'd read my stuff! I knew you right away from your author photo, but I guess since I never include one, you had no way of recognizing me, and I had no reason to think you would!"

"I'm a huge fan of your work. I thought you'd be a bit older than I am, though. Guess that's what happens when you leave your face a mystery." She laughed, "I am, though. Older than you'd guess." Staring off into the shadowy trees, I open up. "Your book is ultimately what gave me the confidence to start submitting pieces." I grin sheepishly, "no wonder I didn't feel shy around you..." She smiles back. Have her teeth always been so pronounced?

Chill wind whips through fall leaves, sending red jewels earthward as twilight drops into night. Seeing me shiver, she opens the thermos, sending spirals of cinnamon steam to join cold breath between us. She pours me a cup, the mug shaped like a jack-o-lantern. The rich mulled cider fills me with unfamiliar warmth, a sense of life that I've too long felt on the periphery of, watching from a dissociative distance.

"Aren't you going to have any?"

"I have something...better in mind." They flash another mysterious smile. "Right now, the only thing I need is you." I blush, nearly choking on a clove. She cracks a wider smile, laughing at my awkwardness. Her large canines glint in the glow from candle flames and what little moonlight shines through noctilucent clouds.

We fall silent, still, listening to the wind dance in dry leaves. Her hair floats in the breeze, too, sending a familiar, comforting scent to mix with cider and night air. She smells honeysuckle after a spring rain. My hands clench around the goblet for warmth and grounding because I feel my heart pounding in that special way that being around my two best friends from my hometown felt, before we moved away to the city. Like every detail of this moment of proximity, this relationship, this easy understanding needed to be written in blood, tattooed on my skin, preserved in resin. After a long pause, a distant owl hooting, a sigh, she speaks my thoughts, erasing what little space remained between us.

"This is the first day I've felt alive in aeons,"

"Me too, Hyacinth!" My eyes flash as I stare into hers, dark brown pools reflecting fall foliage. Her pupils expand. She takes my hand, tracing veins under thin skin.

"I want it to last forever."

I'm not sure who said it first, but what happened next is burned into me like the scars at my throat. First they leaned in, whispered in my ear an offer, asked for consent. Vocal and affirmative and enthusiastic, I say "yes!" Then, blushing, I brush my fluffy purple hair out of the way. I've never been really sex repulsed, always pretty neutral on the whole subject, much more interested in finding people to talk to that didn't make me so scared to speak. So, though this will be my first kiss, I'm not sure it will be my last. After all, we have forever to explore the shifting boundaries of squishy friendship.

"Ready?" They ask, voice husky and eyes dark with thirst, with longing that is no less gripping because it doesn't involve nakedness, genitals or anything my parents would recognize as something to worry about their son getting up to.

"I think I've been ready for you for a while now," I blurt out. "You're the one I've been writing to all this time." She gazes into my eyes, knowing that soon she'll watch the life drain out of them only to be relit by the taste of her blood, reborn. Me but more, just like after top surgery. Free.

Her lips are soft ice brushing against the skin above my jugular. I shiver, knowing I'm on the edge of forever, of relishing in change instead of fearing it, of being alone together however that looks. She bites down, hard. The pain is like nothing I've ever known. The time I broke my wrist falling off the bike, even when I snagged my surgical drain on my bedroom door, nothing comes close. I moan. It's beautiful. I scream. It's too beautiful. Chagall paintings and watching the wind in the sycamores. I think I moan their name. I think I drool, saliva mixing with blood. Every nerve ending is overloaded. Writhing, twitching, my fingers finding their hips, holding them tight. This is the only pleasure I'll ever need. So much better than what I saw in porn, trying to be like the other kids. So much better than my fingers. So much better than being alive. My pulse accelerates. I must be losing a lot of blood. It trickles down my throat, collecting in the hollow between collarbones, soaking my sweater. I think this must be what love is like, just in a different direction. My hands lose their grip. I collapse deeper into their kiss. Stars dot my vision, it fades to purple, then to black. My last moment "alive" is pure sensation, the memory of their tongue licking the pools on my sunken chest as they hold a bitten wrist to my slack mouth, letting their blood flow into me like liquid steroids for anaphylaxis. It burns, ghost pepper hot and sweet. I never expected her blood to taste so warm, though I knew it would be irresistible, addictive. How could it not, when her poetry was the only thing strong enough to break through my anhedonia? I died somewhere in that moment, feeling her trickle down my throat. Then I woke up in her arms on the dewy grass, on a grave that might as well say my name, to being best friends forever.

INCORPORATE
THE BEAST

disregard – Melankalia Stambaugh (she/her)

Center stage, blinded by the spotlight
The tattered costume, the flaking face paint
Watch her jump through jagged hoops
Faster now, ignore the bleeding
You will be polite through tear-stained eyes
The floors tilt, the floors sway
We watch her smile through angst and anguish
She knows what she has to do to gain favor
Oh sweetie, you're not sad enough yet
Internally, maybe
But the performance, my darling!
My seething disdain and all of your hurt
Will only keep me lightly entertained
Bring out the prods, now...how many times
Must i stab you before you sob?
You still won't get what you need
You know you won't, but the objective is to try
My job is no fun with no one to belittle
We'll call it...motivation

why do so many feel that charity,
gives them right to parent the poor
they must be physical gifts because
those people
the struggling, the disenfranchised,
why, we can't be left alone with money
we can't be trusted to operate
in our own self interests
we might be lying, after all, we
have been so unsuccessful at life

Prove to me that you are
This desperate
This lacking Prove it.
And then prove it again, and again
And all the while, I will tell you,
In my most irritated and bored tone
That I wish we could help

every day, seeing, hearing deluded people
romanticizing the simplicity of poverty
when nothing of my life is simple
it is astonishing just how much we give up
in an effort to stay alive while being poor
but is it worth it, is it ever fucking worth it
when giving up is easier?
we are told that that kind of thinking is weakness
you have to keep going, aim high, fight to succeed
for fucking what? work your ass off with no time to do
anything enjoyable or restful
anything with an ability to feed your soul
education, enrichment, art
they're for people who are not us
people who had the luck to never get caught
in this maze of grinding gears, these systems
put in place to break us into tiny fragments

Sshhhhh, you hush now
There is help out there
You just have to ask
Ask ask ask ask
Just ask and we'll fix
Everything.
Charity, you know.
Ignore the Cheshire Cat grin.

according to societal standards,
i contribute nothing of value
my life, as i barely live it, is worthless
it is unthinkable that i could get by
on. so. very. little.
well, i certainly don't like to think about it
but, i must be a liar
obviously, i am a deadbeat
scamming
right?

and we wonder why
why mental illness is on the rise
why birthrates have dropped
why so very many
are so very despondent
we wonder
why

Salt

Descend through sunset
Shed my skin into the sea
Selkie, swimming free

Garden's Revenge

A frog in the grass
doesn't know she needs to
hide
from the lawnmower
Blades seek to cut down
wildness
and call it beauty
Flower trap strikes back
Oil from the pretty petals
burns entitled hands

Transformation

Cast away clothes and scarves
from a thrift store sale bin
get snipped and pinned
Needle and thread
sing through forgotten fabric
Each stitch is a breath
Embellishments
Heartbeats
Life begins again for once
unwanted things

—**Christina Lynn Lambert** (she/her)

An Extra Large Helping Of Justice – Jude Deluca (they/them)

"You're fattening me up!"

It's like that meme with that bug guy. Two identical versions, pointing at each other. What was his name? Tarantulo?

Regardless, Jump Shot's thick index finger aimed at Ohm King. Ohm King likewise had his meaty digit, raised like a gun, locked onto Jump Shot. A Mexican standoff. Both arrived at a similar conclusion, which wasn't the only similarity they shared.

Both were redheads. Hotheads. Superheroes.

Both were very, very attractive.

And currently very, very fat.

Thanks to the escapade with the Chronal Void, Ohm King—formerly Ohm Kid—was trapped in the present day. Even worse, the temporal crisis created an entirely new future. With new versions of Ohm Kid and his 27th Century superbuddies.

Others were stranded in this era too. Some might find a way home. Others, like Ohm King, could never return. Atalanta. Maxine Mockingbird of the Mockingbird Brigade. Dr. Dimension. Perdita.

Jump Shot didn't know how he got stuck with Ohm King. The former teen sidekick, once called "Hoop," had to pull his weight as America's Adjudicators' newbie. Ohm King needed someone to help him acclimate to life in this year.

Neither redhead was happy with this arrangement. Jump Shot didn't want to be a babysitter; Ohm King didn't want to be baby sat. It was a tense situation due to their similarities. Emotional. Volatile. Eager to prove themselves. There were differences. Ohm King generated electricity from his body. Jump Shot lacked superpowers but was almost supernaturally athletic and always hit his target.

There was one other difference between them.

"You cook?" Hoop inquired.

"You don't?" Ohm wondered.

"Never had the time for it," Hoop answered as he surveyed the kitchen table's spread awaiting him one morning. It looked okay. Pancakes. Buttered toast. Scrambled eggs. Bacon.

Hoop didn't trust it.

"I'm surprised you can work a stove," Hoop muttered. "You're always complaining how 'backwards' and 'primitive' everything is."

"I can manage a stove just fine. It's not my fault you people haven't figured out 5D entertainment," Ohm huffed. "I mean, it shouldn't take this long to fix climate change either." He caught Hoop warily eyeing a stack of pancakes and poking it with a fork.

Ohm folded his muscular arms over his chest as he waited for Hoop to sample the food. With a cautious sniff (which elicited Ohm to roll his eyes), Hoop brought a piece of syrup-drenched pancake to his lips.

He chewed. Swallowed.

"Oh!" Hoop was pleasantly surprised. "It's good."

"That's what I was going for," Ohm snarked and calmly ate as Hoop dug in with enthusiasm.

By the end of breakfast, Hoop felt stuffed.

"Where'd you learn to cook?" Hoop wondered aloud as he helped clean up (without being asked).

"I grew up on a farmstead," Ohm casually explained. "My parents taught us to cook and clean for ourselves."

"Us?"

"My siblings. There were nine of us. I was oldest."

Ohm stopped after realizing what he said, dropping a plate into the sink. He didn't notice the soapy water splashing onto his bare, chiseled chest.

Placing a hand on his roommate's broad shoulder, Hoop asked "Are you—?"

"Yeah," Ohm sighed. "I...hadn't thought about it. They're all gone. I *knew*, but..."

"I'm sorry," Hoop sincerely apologized. "I didn't mean to—"

"I know."

"Do you—" Hoop tried to think of what to say. "You wanna tell me about them?"

"Not now, but thank you," Ohm smiled. The first genuine smile Hoop had seen on his scruffy face. It was cute.

"Hey man, thank YOU for cooking" Hoop laughed, "I haven't had a homecooked meal that good in— ever, really."

"You're serious?" Ohm seemed appalled.

"Well, I'm never serious, but yeah, never really had a home growing up," Hoop casually explained. "It's always kind of been me."

Ohm didn't know what to make of that. He sounded so flippant. Ohm couldn't imagine not having a family. Or being alone. Even though technically he was alone *now*. He regarded Hoop's carefree attitude with a sense of sadness.

"As long as I'm here I'll take care of meals," Ohm decided. "It's the least I can do. I know you didn't want to be stuck with me."

"Hey, you wanna cook I'm certainly not complaining." Hoop patted his stomach in anticipation. "Judging from how good breakfast was, I can't wait to see what you have in store for lunch and dinner."

That established a pattern for their living arrangements. If Ohm handled meals, that meant Hoop needed to do some serious shopping. Hoop didn't think about food that much, despite having a sculpted athlete's build which needed serious protein to keep it going while chasing bad guys and stopping supervillains. Ohm was lucky to find what he needed to make breakfast that morning.

"Look, I've spent most of my life living with mentors and teammates," Hoop defended himself after a trip to the local supermarket. "Food's not a thing I had to think about."

"Well, you're thinking about it from now on if I'm cooking," Ohm explained as they filled the fridge and the cupboards. He stopped to examine a box he didn't recall seeing in the shopping cart. He was still trying to process people using paper money, or worse, *crypto*. "What are these?"

"Snack cakes," Hoop took the box and opened it. "Individually wrapped and everything."

"Why are they this color?" Ohm wondered.

"Are you—" Hoop quickly appeared horrified at the sudden thought. "Do they not have junk food in the future? At all?!"

"Yes, there's junk food in the future, dumbass," Ohm argued. "Our tastes are simply more advanced than simplistic caveman desires for—" he scrunched up his face as he read aloud "'Mega Atomic Sugar Cakes With Radical Razzberry Frosting.' The hell? What's a 'razzberry?'"

"You've never eaten junk food before, have you?" Hoop found this hilarious.

"I have so!" Ohm's face was starting to turn as red as his hair while Hoop kept laughing. He didn't know why this was so funny, and Ohm didn't know why he felt sensitive about it as sparks formed at his fingertips.

"Okay, okay," Hoop tried to calm down when he saw how electrified Ohm was getting, before pulling out a cupcake and saying "Here, try it." Ohm hesitated, before he remembered Hoop scrutinizing breakfast earlier in the day. Not wanting to be called a hypocrite, Ohm took the cupcake, unwrapped it, and took a bite.

He chewed.

He swallowed.

He said nothing.

"Well?" Hoop waited for a response. "Do you—?" He found himself cut off when Ohm placed a hand on his shoulder. Ohm's eyes slowly widened; he was experiencing a divine revelation. Hoop couldn't help but wonder if he was hearing "Ode To Joy" playing as Ohm devoured the rest of the cupcake.

Hoop regretted not having his camera out for the moment, especially when Ohm asked once more what a "razzberry" was.

That set the tone for the next several weeks. Things were slow in the hero business. A lot of the typical costumed crooks and world conquerors were laying low ever since the Chronal Void incident. It was as if they looked into the eye of God, and God stared right back. That left your average, non-super crime to deal with. Bank robbers, hijackers, terrorists, serial killers. The usual. Still, Jump Shot and America's Adjudicators weren't as busy as they normally were, which gave Hoop more time to keep an eye on his houseguest.

They developed a bond shared through consumption. Ohm cooked breakfast, lunch, and dinner. In return Hoop kept the cupboards stocked with an assortment of snack cakes and junk food as thanks for Ohm's efforts.

Ohm asked questions about what sort of dishes Hoop preferred while trying to replicate recipes from the future. Thankfully, Ohm wasn't allergic to any foodstuffs from this era so he had no problem taste testing and correcting his cooking where needed. He was turning into a real home body; even packed lunches for Hoop's Adjudicator meetings. Hoop had been embarrassed at first, until he saw the jealous expressions of Starflare, the Yellow King, and yes, even that chronic hardass, Vacuumman. They could tell Hoop's lunches were prepared with love. That envy almost drove them mad when he refused to share a taste.

Hoop remembered Ohm favored snack cakes, mini-pies, cupcakes, toaster pastries, sponge cakes with cream filling. He literally screamed in terror when shown a bag of cheese puffs, exclaiming Earth was being invaded by a race of brain-eating worms, and zapped the bag into dust. That one incident aside, Ohm admitted he was entranced by the variety of snacks and treats found on Earth in this era. He didn't know there were so many ways to wrap up processed sugar.

Slowly, Hoop and Ohm got to know each other beyond their initial assumptions. The more they indulged their appetites, the more they learned. Hoop was blasé about his life as an orphan to the point of having no interest in ever knowing who his birth parents were. He'd spent years bouncing from orphanage to orphanage before his natural athleticism got him adopted by sporting goods heir Oleander "Andy" Knickerbocker, who turned out to be the Jade Javelin.

"He was your dad?" Ohm asked one evening while the two were vegged out on the couch watching reruns of *The Justice Gals* and eating a homemade spinach and goat cheese pizza.

"Dad? He wanted everyone to think that, but Andy was more a pal," Hoop said before a dark look appeared on his face. "Now we aren't even really that."

"What happened?"

Hoop shrugged. "Tale as old as time. Went broke in the recession, had a midlife crisis, and disappeared for like a year to 'find himself.' As if there was much to find. He came back expecting everything to be like it was and it pissed me off. He took me into his home, turned me into his little sidekick, then abandoned me with almost nothing to support myself."

"What'd you do?"

"Punched him in the face. He acted all proud saying how grown up I was, so I kicked him in the balls for good measure."

"Is that it?" Ohm wondered.

Hoop grunted as he reached forward for another slice of pizza, the waistband of his shorts digging into his not-quite chiseled stomach. "He got his fortune back eventually. One of his business partners turned out to be his archenemy, the Money Shark, and had stolen it all. After he was rich again, Andy paid for my school and college. He sends me cash whenever I need it, but that's about it."

Ohm tried to take all that in as he helped himself to the last slice, but Hoop's words made the food taste like ashes. Anyone could see the athletic redhead was trying to distance himself from his crappy upbringing by acting so nonchalant about it. It was sad, really. Of course, Ohm had his own demons he didn't want to deal with, so who was he to throw stones?

A few nights after their discussion about Andy Knickerbocker's less-than-stellar parenting, Hoop, exhausted from a fight with the Devil's Advocates, woke to the sound of sobbing. His footsteps thudded on the hardwood floor as he found Ohm curled up in bed, his sobbing face buried into a pillow.

This was the first time he'd ever seen his houseguest cry.

"H-hey," Hoop reached out to Ohm. "What's—?"

"They're gone!" Ohm sobbed. "They're gone and *I can't take it anymore!*"

"Oh geez," Hoop scratched the back of his head before sitting down on the bed. "I knew this would happen."

"Well good for you for being psychic," Ohm shouted. "Because I sure as Hell didn't expect everyone I loved getting wiped from existence!"

Hoop sat there and listened to Ohm cry as the weight of the last several months finally hit the future hero. He was afraid of Ohm losing control of his powers, but to the future hero's credit not a single stray bolt or spark escaped from his sobbing form. Hoop watched Ohm's broad shoulders tremble and shake until finally he sat up, red-eyed and looking as though his beating heart had been ripped from his large chest.

"It's not even like they're dead, or I could find a way to bring them back" Ohm confessed. "This is *worse* than death. They're *gone*. They never existed. My entire family. My team. M-my friends." The tears kept falling. "Rock Star and Psybelle. IQ and Ghostina. Helium and Dingo and Cordite. Now there's new versions of them. A-a new version of ME. But *I'm* still here. I, I can't," Ohm sobbed. "Why? Why me and not them?"

Hoop didn't know how to answer. Couldn't begin to comprehend the nightmare Ohm was living through. All he did was place a thick arm around the other redhead, letting him cry as much as he needed. Ohm buried his face into Hoop's chest and sobbed to his heart's content, not stopping until the storm he'd been keeping inside of him ran its course.

Neither one remembered falling asleep together. Come morning things had changed.

Hoop made breakfast this time. Though the eggs were a bit runny, and the toast was burnt, Ohm quietly ate without complaint. Didn't say a word throughout the entire meal. That especially bothered Hoop.

"Thank you," Ohm finally said to break the silence when he was done.

"Don't thank me, this wasn't—"

"I meant for last night."

Neither spoke again. The air was heavy with tension when Hoop finally heard "Grayle."

"What?"

"Grayle," Ohm revealed. "My real name."

"Oh. Oh!" Hoop couldn't believe it. "All this time I've called you 'Ohm!' I thought that was your only name, I'm sorry!"

"It's fine," Ohm sighed. "I didn't say anything. It," he gulped. "It's the first time I've said it out loud since I got stuck here."

"Ricky."

"Huh?"

"That's MY real name," Hoop offered. "I've gone by 'Hoop' for so long I don't think about it much."

"Ricky," Ohm repeated.

"Grayle," Hoop addressed.

The tension slowly abated, and without saying a word, the two redheads went back to bed and didn't leave for the rest of the day.

It was clear to everyone Hoop and Ohm—Ricky and Grayle—were now roommates *and* lovers. Everyone had been shocked, a remorseless hound dog like Jump Shot was in a committed relationship. Supposedly. No one had much faith it would last given his track record. Jump Shot had a number of past lovers under his considerably straining belt. Daisy Chain. Princess Peregrine. March Hare. At least one of his ex-girlfriends, Aura, was annoyed at how seemingly devoted he was to Ohm King. Granted, she couldn't recall if she ever dated Hoop in this current life she was living so maybe this shouldn't have surprised her. Reincarnation sucked.

Ohm finally accepted he was permanently living in this era. He began receiving therapy to sort his feelings of grief and survival. Hoop supported him, took the time to listen to Ohm's stories about the future. Refusing to talk about his old life had done Ohm too much damage, so Hoop could tell it was important for him to feel comfortable speaking about his memories. He also made sure they never went without Ohm's favorite snacks. He'd underestimated how much comfort Ohm drew from those treats, and if they helped him deal with his trauma, Hoop made sure they were never without.

It was Ohm who convinced Hoop to give therapy a chance to address his abandonment complex. As someone who had no chance of ever seeing his parents, siblings, or friends again, he admitted to feeling jealous that Hoop's mentor was still alive. That Andy, Jade Javelin, whatever he was called, had no trouble ensuring Hoop had whatever money he needed, showed he must've still cared about his ward in some capacity.

Though he joked about it, Hoop feared legitimately discussing how his mentor and father figure treated him. And he wasn't going to assume anything about Andy's feelings. Giving money from a distance was the bare minimum the guy could do if he wanted to keep Hoop in his life. But, you know, it wasn't like things had been *entirely* bad. There were still good times, even if the bad times outweighed them. Did he *owe* it to Andy? Hoop didn't know. All he knew was if Ohm could confront his own trauma, maybe...

While Ohm watched Hoop struggle with his own emotions, he tried to be there for him as Hoop had given him support. Ohm poured himself into his cooking, preparing each meal with tender love and care. He thought about his old home and his parents, growing up on the farm with all his siblings. Thought about his adventures with Rock Star and Psybelle, his first loves. He took those memories and tried to instill them in every dish he fed to Hoop. If Hoop hadn't been lucky enough to grow up with a family and friends like Ohm had known, this was the best he could do to share those feelings with him.

"I never really said thank you properly," Ohm suddenly said one evening as he brought out a red velvet cake with handmade cream cheese frosting.

"Huh?" Hoop was confused. "Sure you did, you—"

"I mean," Ohm interjected as he sliced a big wedge, "had I been sent anywhere else I would've probably been studied and probed."

"Well," Hoop smirked. "I'd say I've been doing quite a bit—"

"Dumbass," but Ohm laughed anyway. "You didn't treat me like some sideshow freak because I'm from the future. Never asked me questions about history or disasters. Even when I got confused over things, you never made a big deal of it. Oh sure, you teased and joked, but you never made feel ashamed. It—it helped a lot."

What was that jolt, that spark, as Hoop placed a hand over Ohm's while accepting his plate? It was something neither of them would forget.

The following day after their little heart-to-heart, Ohm felt ready to get back into the field as an active superhero. He didn't want to change his codename. He was still Ohm King. Still lived a life in the future, even if some other kid would call themselves Ohm King eventually.

There was just one small (depending on how you looked at it) problem with that.

Hoop had taken a leave of absence for a few months to really help Ohm process his emotions. That's not all they did, mind you. Wink, wink. It was decided Jump Shot and Ohm King would make their grand reentry in the field together. That's when they noticed the BIG change.

On the day Ohm suited up again, he found to his shock he *couldn't.* He had his original Ohm King costume, repaired long ago, in a drawer in Hoop's apartment. Squeezing into the suit was difficult. Tight. Uncomfortable, even. The fabric struggled to contain him, and even after he wedged himself in, he encountered a second trial in buckling his belt. It was a struggle which lasted a small eternity until Ohm finally clasped it shut. If only he hadn't exhaled, at which point *SNAP*.

Frustrated, horrified, Ohm tried to bend over to pick up the broken buckle when he realized his feet were obscured from his vision. He huffed and tried to find the missing piece of his costume when he finally called out "Hoop, I need some help in here!"

"I'm, uh, having some problems of my own," Hoop called back.

When Ohm tried to leave the room and bumped into Hoop—belly first—the two finally realized what happened. All those home cooked meals from Ohm, all those store-bought treats from Hoop, and the lack of exercise (outside of the bedroom) had made the two gain a considerable amount of weight.

Ohm's costume was exceptionally form-fitting, highlighting all his new curves. Hoop's costume of a pair of mesh shorts and a sports jersey did little to hide his girth. His shorts were stretched as far as they could go, but his belly hung firmly over the waistline. The jersey was tight on Hoop's bulky midsection, while his thick, meaty arms were exposed.

This was the first moment either man had realized how much the other had bulked up. They'd spent so much time living together, enjoying each other's company, that they hadn't stopped and noticed their clothes shrinking, their weight increasing.

Their attractiveness multiplying.

Both appeared to have their new thickness distributed evenly throughout their bodies, being neither bottom nor top heavy. Their faces equally plump and round with double chins. Their pectoral muscles now breasts. Their bellies big and round. Their backsides doughy and plush. They simply looked like sturdier, fatter versions of the men they'd always been.

Which brought them to make accusations against the other.

"No wonder you wanted do all the cooking!" Hoop accused as he marched up to Ohm, still pointing an accusatory finger, his belly shifting and hitting up against Ohm's causing him to back up.

"I should've known you had an ulterior motive for getting me to try that cupcake!" Ohm argued, asserting himself against Hoop as his stomach knocked against Hoop's. "Razzberries are probably poisonous aren't they?!"

"FOR GOD'S SAKE IT'S JUST RASPBERRY SPELLED WITH TWO ZS IT'S A PLAY ON WORDS USED FOR ADVERTISING!"

The two heroes fumed at each other, almost as livid as they'd been when they first met. Their round faces turned red as their no longer chiseled jaws clenched in anger. Their guts squished against each other, neither backing down.

They looked like two sumo wrestlers ready to charge at each other.

They both looked like big, angry marshmallows.

They both started laughing.

"You weren't doing this on purpose?" Hoop finally asked.

"No!" Ohm clarified. "Were you?"

Hoop shook his head.

"What do we do now?" Ohm wondered.

Hoop assessed Ohm's round body, as Ohm took in Hoop's. Seeing that there was so much of the other man made them look so much more desirable to each other. Neither one of them had ever had a fetish for food, or eating, or weight, but both carried their bulk so well it made them feel enamored all over again.

To Ohm, he was seeing the results of all his hard work on Hoop's body. If there was a physical representation of the emotions he tried to put into his hard work, it would've been Hoop's belly. To Hoop, he was seeing the effects of him trying to give Ohm some comfort while being trapped in such a strange time.

They decided their superhero re-debut would wait. First, they'd get back into bed. Later, ice cream.

The world could wait for the debut of the new and improved Jump Shot and Ohm King. For now, this moment belonged to them.

"how are you?"

(i am really struggling but i don't know how to tell you//i don't like who i am anymore and i'm grieving my past self//i can't stop thinking about her and what i could have done to stop it from happening//what if i let them all down//will they all leave me, will i be alone?//i don't think i can trust myself anymore//i need help but i don't know how to ask//my heart hurts when i think about her//i can't get out of my head//i can't stand to be alone but i'm afraid that i'm a burden to my friends//please help me//what if i'm not good enough//what if i can't find my way back to myself//i love you so much, please don't leave me too)

"i'm good, how are you?"

@mysoullaidbare

Girl's A Madhouse – Angel Rosen (she/her)

bothersome girl getting unbetter / now
the interrupted bettering / assigned a martyr
at last, underfoot

better in an extra-strength gel capsule
better in a cartoon desert mirage
better in a package stamped from Vermont
better in a fourth-grade spelling bee

bothersome girl
reading Rachel McKibbens
making plans to attend a cat funeral
talking about a driver's license
falling in love when it's wholesale
reliving all of the episodes

getting unbetter
        like a trip   down memory lane
making fossils out of lawn gnomes
eating the aquarium rocks
        & saying sorry
I don't fit in the tank   & saying thank you
        for adjusting the light
& saying oh wow   I thought I was getting better
& saying well actually maybe I still am
I think I just live in a madhouse

IS IT NORMAL THAT MY JOINTS ARE IN PAIN AT 24 should i shave my head should i become a youtuber will i be the one to break the family curse are my parents proud of me do i make the people i love happy enough should i learn how to bake pitta should i learn how to bake at all should i switch to a completely dairy free diet should i start buying natto do they even sell natto in rome will i even be in rome for long enough for the answer to that question to be relevant where will i be living this time next year where will i be living this time in 6 months should i learn how to file my taxes or should i just give up and surrender myself to being the sibling that takes care of the parents or should i cash out of my dreams and get out while i still can and will any of this even matter if the world's collective political and financial status which has been in very precarious balance for a long time doesn't get hit by something just bad enough that the whole thing falls down like a house of cards and the world precipitate into nuclear disaster while the rich watch from bitcoin powered casinos on mars and why am i even bothering typing any of this out when I should be doing like ankle stretches for my goddamn fucking joint pain the universe came from nothing are we made of stardust, or made of nothing? how do you fill all this, with something? it took billions of years. how do you fill all this, with something? you got billions of seconds. do you notice beauty? beauty is everywhere or is it nowhere? *when the environment is abundant, organisms lean towards reproduction. when the environment is unlivable, organisms lean towards immortality.* is this how nothing is so close to everything? is this why you say you struggle with existentialism? it's not a struggle it's endurance. it's how when the guards hit you, you ask for more *hit me like my dad* you shout *you are such a man, ju.st like my dad.* the threat to your life gives meaning to resilience. knowing that you will survive. for the joys and pleasures and cigarette hits of dopamine. for   the   modest satisfaction of completing a task. for the company of someone young and pretty. surviving what you shouldn't makes you proud. you don't want kids, you don't want death. for the fear of reincarnation. for the fear of living this all again. for happiness comes and goes, it's not worth chasing. suffering, there is none. no use on holding on to things, no drive to make a difference. what is that? a difference! somehow you know, you're   blessed   with   a   long life.   or   doomed. is this how everything is so close to   nothing? years.   pass   in   a blink. you blink. they don't. how   do   you   fill   all   this   with   nothing?

My Friends Say – Devon Webb (she/her)

My friends say
I'm loving constantly
they also say
I'm chronically online
both of these things
are objectively
& fundamentally true

Sometimes I wonder
if I should be less trusting
& share less of myself with the internet
the situation is that I probably should
but......I can't
& I don't really want to

I'm sorry wolves
I'm just such a pretty lamb
like that meme
you know the one
I make such a stunning martyr

& I love ego
not narcissism, mind you
but ego
& I don't think enough people understand
the difference between the two

& I love being me
& I love tweeting things like
they're important
like other people will find them
important

like oh my god I'm so audacious it's revolutionary
I'm so fucking annoying!! it sells
I am such a generous
micro internet celebrity

sorry!! I can't help being
well-endowed in my particular brand of
obnoxious autism
is it a sin!!
to be so fucking interesting

is it bad behaviour
to love myself
& these little people in my phone screen
I've never perceived in the flesh

it is impractical,
perhaps
but if we're speaking of morality
I think policing identity is
......well

I think vulnerability
is the thing we should return our
concept of strength to
do you know how empowering it is
to keep healing

to stand tall in the poppy field while
everyone else is either
asleep,
or trying to cut you down

to wear your heart on your sleeve
where people try to pick at it
but you're a masochist
so you feel the prick
& write a poem about it

My Bipolar Medication and Babies or not Babies – Kim Malinowski (she/they)

How do I tell my not boyfriend that sex scares me?
How even if he assured me that he would never lay with me
or hold me—
could I let my body's betrayal still
my quaking, frantic excuses flying into his eyes?

How my guilt drips my body can bear children
when most of my friends cannot carry.
How selfish, not willing to leave behind sanity,
medications flinging and flying away, withdrawal,
and in three months, if not dead by overdose,
I could conceive.
I'm sure that would be pure

        manic

                depressive

                        bliss.

But for family, for my man, for the child—
        technically, I could do this.

After nine months, if I had not hung myself,
if my partner or required, my husband,
had been attentive, not even leaving to pee,
there would be a child.
I would stagnate away from medication another
three months, more, breastfeeding,
if postpartum depression did not kill me.

Can a loving husband even hold my clawing,
beating wrists for over a year,
my writhing and screaming,
so that he and I may hold a child?

Now, if we lay, even in matrimony, and the condom breaks,
he will ask—don't you take birth control?
And I will rapidly, desperately, explain it does not work.
No. Guarantees. Doctors. Said. Be Careful. My. Medications.

And the doctors. I know they hoped I would die before I had sex.
I know that I thought I would die before worrying about carrying cruelty.
A child that could not be born.
A child that could not survive outside hospital even in adulthood.
My medication slowly killing it, defiling its membranes.
And I would love that child. And I would love that man.
But I would be dead within days by my own hand.

*First Published in Ink & Marrow

The Predator Complains – Devon Neal (he/him)

This whole idea of "Antelope Rights"
just isn't feasible.
After all, what do they expect
when they flaunt their flexing thighs
while they graze in the field?
It's the natural order of things
that I use them to satiate my hunger,
especially the most vulnerable of them.
It's not an easy thing, after all,
being at the top of the food chain.
How else am I expected to survive,
or teach my sons how to hunt?
Who is thinking about my rights?
Where I will sleep tonight?
Or how difficult it is to drink from the pond
when any craggy log could have teeth?
If we're talking about rights,
tell me if I'm right or wrong
to feel the gnaw of hunger as they gallop out there.
Isn't it their fault for coming into my territory
and wearing such appealing stripes on their skin?
I just don't know what you expect me to do
when I have so much golden land to cover,
so much power to claim.

COVERING A BLACK WALL WITH AN OUNCE OF WITE-OUT

(THINGS PEOPLE HAVE SAID TO ME)

– **Shannon Clem** (she/they)

Ghazal About My Mirror – Alex Carrigan (he/him)

—After Sarah Ghazal Ali and Dior J. Stephens

I find myself looking in mirrors once again
in hopes my reflection doesn't smile back again.

He looks like he's got shivs coming out of his gums,
with streaks of silver always drooling down his chin again.

He'll cock his head in response to my confusion, his smile lines
turning red as his cheeks begin to gain their color back again.

He taps his finger on the glass like a child at an aquarium,
each time the glass warps a bit over and over again.

I am comforted that he can't escape from the mirror,
but that fear finds its way down my spine again and again.

I'm tempted to stand before the mirror tomorrow and
see if he will deign to show me that smile of his again.

But I know the Alex within that mirror will always smile,
because he knows he successfully lured me in once again.

imagine, if you will, that i am dissociating – nat raum (they/them)

this is disjointed this is fragmented this is coded this is unclear this is called dissociation and if you think i can explain it while caught in the troughs of its relentless swell, then honey, you've got a big storm coming. i am a dripping wound of a human right now. i am a body of shame. i am a genderless ghost seeking revenge. i am a ball of angst and apathy. i perspire in my sleep even with the air conditioning on and all the blankets thrown off in fury or fear. i consider my brain still under refurbishment. this is listless. this is the tangled mass my favorite gauze-pop singer spoke of. this is *i am not dead just floating*[46] this is *but i wish i was sometimes* this is all i've known for half a year now. this is a mist finer than fog and i am adrift without lanterns. without maps. without the whole motor for fuck's sake. i am waiting out the weather because this is an *all summer in a day* type situation: if i do not see the sun soon, i will die here in an overcast twilight.

First published in BRUISER

---

[46] italicized is a lyric from P!nk's "I'm Not Dead"

Digging Through the Trash – Shannon Clem (she/they)
(Dumpster Diver Theme)

I've gotta quit digging through the trash,
my mother says.

But I only feel at home in a dumpster.

Banana peel in hair.
Scum stuck between fingers.
Rat scurrying over my thumb—
Me, trapped under...

Somewhere some motherfucker
sucks up a shucked oyster,
licking lemon-sticky fingers,
using hundreds as napkins—

With his nose upturned at me.
And there are thousands of him.

How can I feel comfortable
anywhere else?

When a man calls me "fuckin'
retard—"

Tells me I "just need to—"

I say, "Thank you, Daddy—
I'm yours."

Maybe he'll open up the lid
and toss in a watermelon rind—
(Do they eat those at charity dinners?)

And I can look inside the window
while I nibble with my rat-friend—

God knows it understands me
better than him.

Some passers-by
in the Whole Foods parking lot
flirt with whether or not
to call the cops.

They opt to open up
their canvas loot—
Sip kombucha right
from the bottle—
Licking their lips at me.

I imagine an '80s movie:
A stuffy businessman
and a scruffy hobo
swap lives.

Making sure we get
one thing straight—

No one ever dives
in a dumpster
to stay.

A blockbuster comedy.
A feel-good family film.

The tragedy I pull—
In blackened,
slightly dampened,
organic coffee grounds,
from my graying hair—
for breakfast.

come join me
in my apothecary of
dreams

where the biting wind
no longer has teeth
and the ache in your heart
turns to velvet midnight

pastel watercolors abound
as you fall into
bliss-addled reverie

a world of sage and silk
a distant memory come
to life

ophelia monet
@mysoullaidbare

Social Anxiety – Megan Diedericks (she/her)

I walk the line between life and death
(No, this is just a mall, not the thin
stretch of road between the veils.)

I am being stalked
(No, those are just
faces in passing.)

I can barely breathe
(No—wait, that's true,
actually.)

There's a creature waiting to pounce
(No—well, not a physical
monster anyway.)

I am being checked into my death-box
(No, this is a branch of the bank
not molded and shaped tree-branches.)

My heart is hammering, looking for an escape
(No, I think it might just give way
and stop ticking, actually.)

The evil eyes are scorching my soul
(No, I wouldn't know;
I avoid making eye contact.)

My voice is trapped in my throat
(No, because I can feel my mouth moving
but I can't imagine how it sounds.)

They said they couldn't help me
(I didn't ask for help.)

How is it that my words mean so little? – Kim Malinowski (she/they)

That my life means so little?
I am dollars and pennies
and even as I write my prescription costs $1,500
and when I told the receptionist at my psychiatrist's office
that my not covered medication was a death sentence,
she laughed. I sucked in my breath, cut deeper than marrow
and no one cares if I live or die or die trying to live.
I am reflection of multiple positions reading and not able
to read. My future seems to be dropping off a cliff
as drug names are read to me over and over.
I took 1, 3, 5, l, z took away language, my psychiatrist
doesn't remember my brain damage. Have we tried…?
Yes, we tried r, and 2, 4, 6 and a rolodex I don't remember.
I wish my shadow self could take the generic, but my flesh self
cannot. I do not want to die. Not yet. But the chorus
of the you don't matter and the chants of you cost too much to keep
get louder. I hear: you are broken, you are broken.
I refuse to let you break me. I will read and beg and read some more.
Let lightning come. I am ready.

It's Just a Fantasy with Your Face on it – Melina Cohen-Bramwell (he/him)

Transference onto me
Counter onto you
10mg methylphenidate
Addy turning me blue
Billy Fy wants in the door I'll open it for you
I'll open my legs too
Do what you want me to

Don't you like me so why fight me
So why tie me Zombify me
Anti-psy me how could I be
writing these little love notes in a state like this
Tell me your real name I insist Doc
Is it Joey for your friends
Would you blow me if I said
I showered yesterday instead of last week
Smack these rosy little cheeks
I'll make them clap for you
Love how you listen to me speak

When I pay for it by the hour
Write your script so I'm not dour
Write your scripts so that I shower for fucks' sake
Wake up

Poem upon discovering that all of my favorite writers are anorexic – [sarah] Cavar (they/them)

I want to crack an egg at the base of your clavicle & lick
what remains from your teats
Like a young pig.

::

I cannot stand the thought of you
Better at me than I,
cannot stand your skill
Outdoing my skinny.

It is a kind of plagiarism.
Contagion? I fear I have been socialized to hate
The shit I love the most. To believe it not verse
But plot, coup, seize me by the
Tawny weft between my stem and spine.

Of course, I am watching the mirror: warp, lover,
thorn, vengeance, bite.
langue, my most pathetic skin
becomes me.

::

I stand before you w/
my poem wet-toed, naked   afraid
to look down.

I wait for the day my envy shrinks, or I have
the brass to kill it.

I wait for you

                                        Too

- Alex Carrigan (he/him) is a Pushcart-nominated editor, poet, and critic from Alexandria, VA. He is the author of Now Let's Get Brunch: A Collection of RuPaul's Drag Race Twitter Poetry (Querencia Press, 2023) and May All Our Pain Be Champagne: A Collection of Real Housewives Twitter Poetry (Alien Buddha Press, 2022). He has appeared in The Broadkill Review, Sage Cigarettes, Barrelhouse, fifth wheel press, Cutbow Quarterly, and more. Visit carriganak.wordpress.com or follow him on Twitter @carriganak for more info.

- Alexandra Weiss is a writer, plant enthusiast and grad student at the IU Bloomington Liberated Zone for Palestine. Sasha has published three poetry and visual poetry chapbooks: *autumn is when the ghosts come out* (Blanket Sea Press), *obituary for my hot sauce shelf* (Bottlecap Press), and...*but i work here* (Querencia Press). They also make low quality but heartfelt indie pc games as Cerberus Studios on itch.io.

- Angel Rosen (she/her) is a lesbian poet living in Pennsylvania. She's been published by Bullshit Lit, Rogue Agent, Anthropocene, and others. Angel spends her time reading, writing, watching television, and getting bubble tea. She is passionate about destigmatizing mental illness, collaborating in art communities, and trying to be friends with everyone in the world. angelrosen.com & @Axiopoeticus.

- Ariele Costantino aka @cybermaenad (he/they) is a poet, essay writer and digital artist based in Rome, Italy. He is interested in time travel, prophecy, the nature of consciousness, and ways of blending green tea. Their work can be found in Stone of Madness, Memezine, and Sinister Wisdom (forthcoming).

- arushi (aera) rege is a queer, chronically in pain, Indian-American poet in senior year in high school. They tweet occasionally @academic_core and face the perils of instagram @aera_.writes. They are the proud author of exit wounds (no point of entry) and BROWN GIRL EPIPHANY (kith books '24, fifth wheel press '25). They are the EIC of nightshade lit, Bus Talk, and Draupadi Interviews. You can find their website at arushiaerarege.carrd.co.

- Audrey T. Carroll (she/they) is the author of *What Blooms in the Dark* (ELJ Editions, 2024), *The Gaia Hypothesis* (Alien Buddha Press, 2024), *Parts of Speech: A Disabled Dictionary* (Alien Buddha Press, 2023), and *In My Next Queer Life, I Want to Be* (kith books, 2023). Her writing has appeared in Lost Balloon, CRAFT, JMWW, Bending Genres, and others. She is a bi/queer/genderqueer and disabled/chronically ill writer. She serves as a Fiction Editor for Chaotic Merge Magazine and Editor-in-Chief of Genrepunk Magazine. She can be found at http://AudreyTCarrollWrites.weebly.com and @AudreyTCarroll on Twitter/Instagram.

- "Hey lady, you, lady; Cursing at your life....." Beppi wonders if shuffle or an AI generated mix is doing her dirty on her pensive car rides. Her Subaru is frequently where the magic happens. (Next) "You're on a mission & you're wishing'; Someone could....." (Next) The haunting notes of "Dies Irae" sound.... Wow, That is gonna spark something. Beppi's mind sparks. Images form. Beppi yells, "Mutha fucka, let me in!"

- Brendon Blair is an Appalachia-born writer born and bred on trailer living and warm Mexican cuisine. As a recent dual graduate of Psychology and English, Brendon enjoys intertwining the experiences of queer, waifed and fostered people in poetry and prose. They work as the assistant chapbook editor for Sundress Publications and are passionate about accessible learning. You can find out more at @poxpoet on Tiktok or @poxpoet on Instagram.

- Christina Lynn Lambert writes romance novels, science fiction, horror, and poetry. Her stories and poems are about fighting for change, the beauty of nature, and trying to find the good moments in life. She lives in beautiful Virginia with her family.

- Devon Neal (he/him) is a Kentucky-based poet whose work has appeared in many publications, including *HAD, Stanchion, Stone Circle Review, Livina Press,* and *The Storms,* and has been nominated for *Best of the Net* in 2023 and the Pushcart Prize in 2024. He currently lives in Bardstown, KY with his wife and three children.

- Devon Webb (she/her) is an autistic writer & editor based in Aotearoa New Zealand. Her award-winning work, concerning themes of femininity, anticapitalism & neurodivergence, has been published extensively worldwide & accumulated six Best of the Net/Pushcart nominations. She is a founding member of The Circus (@circuslit), a literary collective prioritising radical inclusivity in the indie lit scene. She is currently working on her debut novel & full-length poetry collection, & can be found on social media at @devonwebbnz.

- Dia VanGunten writes unhinged fiction and makes bad decisions like dancing in platform disco boots or strutting on uneven surfaces. She falls on her ass and makes a fool of herself. She is a tightrope walker wobbling across the last strand of angel hair pasta. She is a row boat on the nose of a dolphin, a rhino on roller skates and a fart that can't be trusted. "There was preserved in her the fresh miracle of surprise." James Douglas Morrison

* Eileen E. was born and raised in a little suburb just west of Covina that resides on Gabrielino-Tongva land. Eileen writes about grief in between writing about hope, mostly in the form of poetry and speculative fiction. Eileen and a few cool comrades will be creating podcasts as the Generic Podcast Group.

* Emily Rose Miller (she/they) is currently earning her MFA in creative writing at the University of Central Florida. Their work has been published in Saw Palm and Cagibi Lit, among other places. Find them online at emilyrosemiller.com or on Instagram @emily.rose.miller.

* ezel (he/they) is a queer poet living in Istanbul. Their work appears at velvele, Orlando Poetry Art, and devedikeni and is forthcoming at Orlando's 2024 pride month anthology. He can be found on Instagram @centerofthings.

* Gwendolyn Harper (She/They) sometimes writing as the Maenad is the author of The Ishtar Cycle (2021), and Flying the Jolly Scarlet Gambling with the Gods (2023) Their anthology work has appeared in True Grit, Bone Milk Vol 2 and Vulcanalia 21. Work has appeared at ZiN Daily, Writers Resist, 365 Tomorrows, the World History Encyclopedia, Beyond the Underground, and Cream Scene Carnival. She has also been published in the Fahmidan Journal, Corporeal, Troublemaker Firestarter, and Engendered. Columnist at Cream Scene Carnival. Founder / Publisher Dreaming Gynoid Studio Best of fhe Net Nominee 2023 Co-founder and former editor of Viridian Door. Has read for Farside Review Founder / Publisher Dreaming Gynoid Studio, author of the Galaxy Black RPG. Editor & Publisher of Sub-ether. A queer, disabled, angry punk Goddess, Gwendolyn writes about trauma, sex, politics, pop culture, science fiction, history, space, and sex work. They have lived experience of homelessness, intimate partner violence, drug abuse and addiction as well as a childhood of family, institutional, and medical abuse. Insta @scarlet_Maenadum

* HJ Farr (they/them) is a multidisciplinary artist, combining dramatic training from a lifetime in Musical Theatre with their own solitary ponderings on queerness, gender, mental health, mundane tiny things, and the world at large. Along with writing, HJ also acts, performs circus, sews, and tries to keep up with societal issues in which they may be able to make things a little bit better. You can find their daily poetry at kipventures.poetry.blog, life-things @hjenby on the 'gram, and their very first short story published in the 8th edition of Brave New Girls!

* Irina Tall (Novikova) is an artist, graphic artist, illustrator. She graduated from the State Academy of Slavic Cultures with a degree in art, and also has a bachelor's degree in design. The first personal exhibition «My soul is like a wild hawk» (2002) was held in the museum of Maxim Bagdanovich. In her works, she raises themes of ecology, in 2005 she devoted a series of works to the Chernobyl disaster, draws on anti-war topics. The first big series she drew was The Red Book, dedicated to rare and endangered species of animals and birds. Writes fairy tales and poems, illustrates short stories. She draws various fantastic creatures: unicorns, animals with human faces, she especially likes the image of a man – a bird – Siren. In 2020, she took part in Poznań Art Week. Her work has been published in magazines: Gupsophila, Harpy Hybrid Review, Little Literary Living Room and others. In 2022, her short story was included in the collection «The 50 Best Short Stories», and her poem was published in the collection of poetry «The wonders of winter».

* J.S. NicShuibhne is a Melungeon author with an M.F.A. from McNeese State University. She has been published once before in the cryptid anthology It Came from the Swamps by Malarkey Books, and currently survives by living in a basement and subsisting off the occasional lost pet.

* Jessica Swanson (she/her) lives somewhere along Florida's Nature Coast. She has had work published with *Fifth Wheel Press*, *Voidspace Zine*, and others. She has a fondness for cats, cheese, and fancy tea leaves. Find her on Instagram at everystupidstar and Twitter at Cooljazsheepie.

* john compton (b. 1987) is gay poet who lives in kentucky with his husband josh and their dogs and cats. his latest full-length books are "the castration of a minor god" published with Ghost City Press [now a pdf version] (dec 2022) and "my husband holds my hand because i may drift away & be lost forever in the vortex of a crowded store" published with Flowersong Press (dec 2024); his latest chapbook is "melancholy arcadia" published with Harbor Editions (may 2024).

* jp thorn is a queer, neurodivergent artist raised in & returned to the south. you'll usually find them in a peaceful flow state of adhd hyperfocus or ping-ponging between cat parent & hobbyist. advocate of de-stigmatization & radically-open communication, their work is largely inspired by humanness, reframing traditionalism, therapeutic processes, unlearning patriarchy, identity, & global patterns. you can find more of their work http://thorn.jp/, as well their personal instagram @jpeeperz

* Jude Deluca's a nonbinary aegosexual Capricorn (he/him/they/them). Their areas of interest are magical girls, slasher fiction, YA horror, superhero dads, and big beautiful men. As a professional horror detective they've rediscovered and uncovered several lost and unpublished stories from the 1990s. They can be found on Twitter as @judedeluca1990 and on Instagram and Tumblr as @judedeluca

* Kim Malinowski is a lover of words. Her collection Home was published by Kelsay Books and her verse novel *Phantom* Reflection was published by Silver Bow Publishing. *Buffy's House of Mirrors* was published by Q, an imprint of Querencia Press. She has two more books

forthcoming. She was nominated for the Pushcart Prize, Best of the Net, and the Rhysling Award. She writes because the alternative is unthinkable.

* Lawrence Miles is a poet living in White Plains, NY. He has recently been published in New Feathers Anthology 2023, Bombfire and Up Your Ars Poetica. More of his work is available at lawrence,miles.substack.com.

* Marie Elizabeth Thomas is a queer writer and poet living on the outskirts of Pittsburgh, Pennsylvania. Her article on Catholic homeschooling and abuse was featured by US Catholic last year, and her poetry has been published by the Ethel Zine, Flipped Mitten Press, and Appartition Lit, which nominated her poem "Apples in Hell" for the Pushcart Prize. You can find more of her work on her website, marieelizabeththomas.com.

* Megan Diedericks writes poetry and fiction, everything from meek to macabre can be found in between the lines. Her debut poetry collection: "the darkest of times, the darkest of thoughts" is available on Amazon. Find her on Instagram: @meganreflects!

* Melankalia Stambaugh (she/her) is.................................. confused? Chaotic? Bad at writing bios? Yes. A former small town Ohioan and now trying to navigate big city Oregon, Melankalia is a fiber artist, avid photographer, and unashamed "insta-poet" (@lifevsmelankalia),, who writes largely on the subjects of grief, mental illness, poverty, and nature.

* Melina Cohen-Bramwell, he/him, is a writer and lifelong San Francisco Bay Area resident who also happens to be a biracial, gender-queer, spoonie. Never a fan of the education system, at age sixteen, Melina dropped out of school and began a career in theater. After years of working as a technician at regional theater companies such as Aurora, Cal Shakes, and Berkeley Rep, Melina "retired" to focus on healing from chronic illness and pursuing writing as a profession. His play, Please Don't Slow Me Down, was workshopped in PlayGround SF's summer 2023 Free Play Festival. His play One of the Good Ones, was read in 2022 at Theatre Battery and in PlayGround SF's 2024 Free Play Festival. Buy his book, Bar Fights with Sad Kids, available from Finishing Line Press.

* nat raum is the poet laureate of the void. They can be found online at natraum.com

* Of Thousands is a queer Wisconsin transplant residing in Chicago. They're inspired by their found family, fashion, and the intersection of city and nature, working daily in mixed media.

* Ophelia Monet (she/her) is an educator, mother, and storm chaser, living in Kentucky with her husband and their son. Her work is forthcoming in *Free Verse Revolution, Unleash Lit, Loud Coffee Press, Heimat Review, The Orchards Poetry Journal*, and more. You can find her on Instagram at @mysoullaidbare.

* Rachael Ikins followed her pen into the forest as a child. As with Gretel in the Grimm Brothers' tale, a wicked witch forced her to reroute through valleys so dark she doubted the existence of the sun at times. She lost everything before she finally understood her truth: write like a motherfucker, write or die. For poetry was the constant through all storms, the beloved she refused to relinquish. She won some prizes, published in journals and then books. Weathered downpours of rejections. When last seen Ikins was feeding pickled jalapeños to a large dragon perched on the roof of her house—a dragon who bestowed her name upon Ikins's cat. Sister souls of fire and passion.

* |sarah| Cavar is an anti-genre writer, PhD candidate, and instructor of undergraduates on both u.s. coasts. Their debut novel, Failure to Comply, is forthcoming with featherproof books (2024). Cavar is editor-in-chief of manywor(l)ds.place, and has had work published in The Offing, Split Lip Magazine, Nat. Brut, Electric Lit, and elsewhere. More at www.cavar.club, librarycard.substack.com, and @cavarsarah on twitter.

* Shannon Clem (she/they) is a queer, neurodivergent, disabled anomaly residing with their daughter in California. Shannon's work is featured in various journals & anthologies including *The Hunger, Beaver Magazine, Bullshit Lit, Anti-Heroin Chic, Not Ghosts, But Spirits Vol. III* (Querencia Press), *Reformatting the Pain Scale* (Olney Magazine), & more. Find them at shannontantrum.com.

* William Roberds-King is an autistic trans man living in the PNW with his husband and their two cats. He earned a Bachelor's in English (Creative Writing) at Eastern Washington University. You can occasionally find him on Bluesky at @chaoticfall.bsky.social, Twitter at @chaotic_fall, or Instagram at @fiberwitchwilliam.

* Zo Copeland (they/them) is a writer from Devon, UK. They are inspired by their lived experiences of queerness and disability, and by their magical experiences in nature. Zo writes to connect with people, evoke change, and challenge taboo subjects. Their work can be found with Querencia Press, Arachne Press, Dark Thirty Poetry Publishing, and Big White Shed @zocowrites

www.ingramcontent.com/pod-product-compliance
Lightning Source LLC
Chambersburg PA
CBHW081124300726
48977CB00005B/879